MAKING AMENDS

"What are you fellows doing in all those feathers?" Ramona Delpheen asked. She wasn't sure why the butler had let strangers through the door.

The men said nothing. Long robes of yellow feathers hung down to their knees. One of them carried what appeared to be a phallic symbol made of stone. "We are all of Indian blood—Actatl. All we wished for was to live. But you would not let us. You have violated what we hold precious and worthy, the stone of our ancestors, the life of our hearts, the most gracious and central inspiration of our being."

The next moment, the man with the phallic symbol of stone raised it above Ramona's head and rammed it into her chest. He worked quickly, severing the last arteries, and then with a rip he tore the heart out of her body. Then he left a note with its corners carefully smeared with her blood. She was the second victim . . .

D1602989

The Destroyer

KING'S CURSE #24

by Warren Murphy

PINNACLE BOOKS • LOS ANGELES

THE DESTROYER: KING'S CURSE

An original Pinnacle Books edition, published for the first time anywhere.

ISBN: 0-523-41239-8

First printing, July 1976
Second printing, June 1977
Third printing, April 1978
Fourth printing, April 1979
Fifth printing, May 1980

Cover illustration by Hector Garrido

Printed in the United States of America

PINNACLE BOOKS, INC.
2029 Century Park East
Los Angeles, California 90067

For:

Amnon, Judy, Sharon, Uriyah, Joseph, Gilli, Naomi, Ruthi, and most of all the awesome magnificence of the House of Sinanju.

KING'S CURSE

Chapter One

The stone was old before the pale men on four high legs with metal chests and metal heads followed the path of the sun in from the big water you could not drink.

Before the king-priests, the stone was; before the warrior-kings, it was. Before the Aztec and the Toltec and the Maya, it was. Before the Actatl, who served it and acknowledged it as their own personal god, the stone was.

The stone was a king's height, and if you did not know that the circle outlined in its belly was carved by the very gods themselves before man came from the mouth of the turtle, if you did not know that, then you were not Actatl. And you would not be allowed in the palace of the god, and

1

you would not be allowed near the sacred stone, lest the god be enraged by an unbeliever's finger touching it.

And the people called the sacred stone Uctut.

But only the priests knew its real name.

In the first years of the pale men the warrior king of the Actatl called the five priests of Uctut to the palace, which was 142 steps high and protected Uctut from the north wind and the north light. He asked the priests what they thought of the new pale men.

"Moctezuma says they are gods," said one priest.

"Moctezuma thinks the gods breathe when he vents air after a feast," said the king.

"Moctezuma is a king that is more to god's way," said another priest reproachfully. "It is known that the Aztec of Moctezuma follow their gods better because their king is a priest."

"Life is too short to spend it preparing for its end," the king answered. "And I believe that the rain falls without a baby's heart being thrown into the well that feeds Uctut, and I believe that new babies come even if the hearts of women are not sent into the well, and I believe that I win victories, not because Uctut has been fed with blood, but because my men fight from high places and others from low."

"Have you never wanted to know the name of Uctut? The real name? So that he could speak to you as he speaks to us?" another priest asked.

"What for? Everyone has a name for something. It is just a breath of air. I have not called you here to say that after so many years I have

2

come to your way. Let it remain at this: You give the people your gods, and I do not take the people away from you. Now I ask you, what do you think of the men colored like clouds?"

"Uctut thinks he must have their hearts for his water," said one priest.

"Moctezuma thinks we should give the tall ones with four legs the yellow metals they seek," said another.

And another said, "Moctezuma has also said we should give the hearts of these white men to Uctut."

"Did Moctezuma say the Aztec should give the hearts of these white men with their death sticks?" the king asked. "Or did he say the Actatl should take these hearts?"

"He said it was such a good sacrifice, we should be pleased to make it to Uctut," said a priest.

"Then let the great Moctezuma take their hearts," said the king, "and he may offer them up to Quetzalcoatl, the plumed serpent god."

Another priest responded, "He said the Aztec honored the Actatl by not taking this rich sacrifice for themselves but allowing us to take it for Uctut, to make our god rich and red with the finest hearts."

"Then this I tell to Moctezuma, great king of the great Aztec, from his most respectful neighbor, king of the Actatl, holder of leopards, who protects Uctut from the winds of the north, conquerer of the Umay, Acoupl, Xorec. To Moctezuma, I say, greetings neighbor. We appreciate your generosity and in turn, we give gifts to the Aztec and their great king."

3

While the king spoke, the priests all made sacred marks, for they were knowing of the mysteries, how one man could place a mark on a tablet of stone, and how another man seeing that mark could divine a thought from it, even though the maker of the mark had gone many years before to the other world.

Five hundred years later, in a land where almost everyone read and there was no mystery to it, archaeologists would engage in a favorite pastime of wishing they could talk to inhabitants of the dead cultures they studied. They would say they could get more from a half-hour conversation with someone who lived in that culture than they could get from a lifetime of studying the marks on the tablets they had found.

Yet, if they had talked to the average Actatl, they would have gotten only that the marks were mysteries, that the king lived high, the people lived low, and the priests served Uctut, whose real name only the priests knew and were allowed to speak.

But the stone that was Uctut would last. The Aztec would be no more, the Maya and Inca would be no more. The name of the Actatl would be destroyed, and the Umay, the Acoupl, the Xorec, the inland people they had conquered, would not even be remembered.

All would be forgotten. Yet Uctut would survive and in that far-off time, in a land called the United States of America, blood and horror would be visited upon many, in a royal sacrifice by the Actatl to their god of the stone.

4

And that blood sacrifice started from what happened that day when the king of the Actatl attempted to avoid facing in battle the Spanish invader, whom he suspected was not a god, but just a man of a different color.

And so the priests made their marks and the king spoke. The gift he and his people would give to the Aztec would be the sole rights to the hearts of the pale men on four high legs with metal chests and metal heads.

One priest protested that this was too generous an offer, that Uctut would be jealous of Quetzalcoatl, the Aztec's chief god. But the king signalled for silence and the message was over.

For Uctut's approval a small sacrifice was chosen, a young girl of budding breasts from a fine family, and she was dressed in a royal robe of yellow feathers and placed upon the stone above the well that held the waters that fed Uctut.

Now if her family seemed to be forcing tears and only pretending to wail, there was good reason. For many generations now the Actatl had bought slaves and kept captives for just such a ceremony, and when the priests called for a sacrifice from the ranking soldiers and from those who directed the farmers and the building of roads, they would dress those slaves kept just for this purpose and offer them to Uctut.

One priest held one ankle, and another priest held the other ankle, and two other priests held the wrists. They were strong men of necessity because the bodies struggling for life often had great power. This girl's skin was smooth, and her

5

teeth were fine, and her eyes were shiny black. The fifth priest nodded approvingly at the family, who would be pleased with themselves later; now they lamented as if the child were their own daughter.

With delicate care, the fifth priest unfolded one side of the robe and then the other, and so careful were his hands that the girl smiled hopefully up at him. Perhaps he would let her go. She had heard other slaves say that sometimes they would bring you to the big rock and let you go. Not often but sometimes. And she had placed pebbles in a circle on a grassy bank to the gods of the streams who, while not as strong as Uctut, could sometimes outwit him. And her only request since she had been brought to the special building from the fields was that her god would outwit Uctut and let her live.

And did not the priest's smile above her and his gentle hands mean that he would say this girl is too small and too sweet to die this day? She did not know, nor did the other slaves, that victims were sent back only because of crossed eyes or chipped teeth or scars that would make them unseemly.

But this was a pretty little girl and so the Actatl priest ripped out her heart.

It was a good heart, still pumping in his gentle hands after it was cut and ripped out of the young chest, and she had given a good scream that would increase Uctut's appetite. The priest held the moving heart high so that all would see what a fine gift the family gave for the benefit of all.

The supposed mother wailed and collapsed to

6

her knees in supposed grief. A laudation chant filled the open cathedral of the rock, and before the heart was stilled the priest lowered it to the well, and the four other priests sent the body after, careful that the valuable robe did not go in with it.

Thus was the king's message to Moctezuma assured of the good will of Uctut.

The king watched all this with apparent approval, but his mind was not with the stupid, cruel little ceremony. Even as a little boy he had realized that it was not Uctut who wanted hearts, but the priests and the people. And since the only ones who suffered were slaves and captives, the ceremonies would continue.

He had other things on his mind this day as he looked out upon his people and their homes and fields, which he knew stretched twenty days run in all directions, beyond mountains and rivers and plains. All this was doomed. The people were doomed. Even the very words they spoke would disappear. And while he knew this must have happened to others and would happen to still others and that it was the way of things, some coming and some going, yet inside him something he could not fathom insisted that he not allow this.

He knew the visitors from the water you could not drink would take everything, for they wanted more than the yellow metal and more than slaves. They wanted, according to the king's spies, what they said was in every man and lived forever. Sort of a mind, but not a mind, the spies had said. And they wanted this thing for their god.

And their god was one god, yet three gods, and

7

one had died but had not died. The king had instructed his spy to ask if the pale men's new god would accept a fourth—Uctut—and when the spies returned with the words they had translated from the new language, the king understood that everything the Actatl and the Aztec and the Maya and all the rest had known was over and done. The words were: "You shall have no other gods before me."

This god would not take blood or food or ornaments. He wanted the living minds of his people. Not like Uctut, who could be fooled by a yellow feathered robe and an artificial wail from someone pretending to be a victim's mother.

The king had not mentioned anything to the priests, lest in their fear or anger they attempt something that would surely fail. This new thing was unlike anything the Actatl had ever known, and against it nothing they had ever known would be effective.

That evening of the sacrifice, the king announced he would stay in his high place for many days, but he dressed as a slave, and accompanied by his most fearsome warrior, and he left the high place with a bundle of yellow metal. Now the warrior had much difficulty treating the king as a slave at first, since from birth he had been trained to serve his king and lay down his life to save that of his king. But the king told him that now they must use the deception of rank as their cover, like they used the cover of the forest once. The warrior was puzzled by this as they ran along the roads at night. Everyone knew that the king was a king because he was king. He was not a slave, otherwise he would be a slave. And the pale new-comers would know this, for those who are kings are kings.

Now the king could not tell him what he had long suspected—that the differences in men were made up by men like children's stories were made up, except that differences among men were believed in. So the king told the warrior he had made a magic spell which would make pale men believe he was a slave and not the Actatl king. And this satisfied the warrior.

They ran through the night and in the morning they slept. For twenty-two days they did this, passing the home city of Moctezuma. And one morning they saw a fearful thing.

A pale man, twice as tall as other men, with much hair on his face and shiny metal on his head and chest, and two legs fore and two behind, walked past them, and instinctively the warrior shielded his king. But the king warned him again that he was to be treated as a slave, not a king, and there would be no more warnings. He could not give him another warning.

And they walked out of their hiding place and the tall pale man pointed at them a spear without a point but with a hole in it. And the king noticed that there was another head the same color as the body, and then he realized why the pale man had four legs and was so incredibly tall. He sat on an animal.

Had not the Inca to the south trained animals to carry bundles? This strange new animal had been trained to carry a man. And the king real-ized the metal was just something that was put on the pale man's head. This was confirmed when they entered a large camp, and the king saw some men with metal on their heads and some men without. He also saw the pale men and the strange animals separated, and not joined together.

He saw a queen of the coastal people sitting on a high chair next to a pale man, and he and the warrior were brought to them. The woman spoke the language of the Aztec, and she spoke to the warrior. As he had been instructed, the warrior gave his name and his function as an Actatl, then waited.

The woman questioned in Aztec and then spoke to the pale man in another language. And the king memorized each sound as it came from her lips for there was much he had to learn to save his people. And then the warrior said he had captured this slave fleeing from the city of Moctezuma.

The warrior paused, and the woman talked the strange language, and while she pronounced Moctezuma correctly, the pale man could not. When he repeated it, he said "Montezuma" with different emphasis.

The warrior said the slave was worthless and had nothing because Moctezuma and the Aztecs were poor. And the woman spoke in the other language, and the pale man spoke, and there was tension in their voices. And the woman said to the warrior that the Aztec was not poor, that Moctezuma himself had rooms of gold. And the warrior said, no gold. Just worthless slaves. And when the woman spoke again, the king of the Actatl, dressed as a slave, let loose the many heavy weights of gold he had run with for many days, and he paid scant attention to them, brushing off his poor rags as though the gold was but the dust of the earth.

And, as he had planned, this caused great commotion, and the pale ones even tried to eat the gold by pressing their teeth into it. And the king pretending to be a slave laughed and cried out: "Oh, great queen, why do these pale ones love the yellow dirt so much?"

"Did this come from Moctezuma's city?" she asked, and the king nodded low like a slave and said, "Yes. It comes from the rooms of gold."

And when she repeated this to the pale one, he jumped up and danced, and from then on the pale man wanted words from the slave and ordered the warrior put to death for telling untruths. And thus was the slave-king trusted and taken into the camp of the pales, and thus did this pale man, whom the king later found out was named Cortez, proceed to his long and difficult siege of Moctezuma's city, finally taking it.

During the months of siege, the king thought to be a slave gave bits of information about the Aztec, like a lake letting only a little stream flow out each day. And he watched and learned. Like his own people, few here could read, although the secrets were not guarded. He learned the new language from a priest of the new god. He learned that it was not the sound from the sticks that killed, but a projectile that came at great speed from a hole in the stick. He learned that there were bigger sticks that fired bigger projectiles.

11

One night he learned to ride a horse and almost got killed.

The pale men's metals were harder than the Actatl's. Their military formations were not superior, but being able to stand twenty to thirty paces off and kill with the sticks called guns, the formations did not have to be superior. Their writing was not symbols of things but symbols of sound, and in this, the Actatl king knew, there was a great power. Lighter people were treated better than darker people, and these pale men did not, as his spies had correctly told him, sacrifice people or animals, although at first when he saw the statue of the man stretched out on crossed bars, he was not sure.

He saw the city of Moctezuma fall and its people enslaved, and he was sure that even as the stronger Aztec were doomed, so were his own people. There would be hardly a trace.

These pale men from a land called Europe were robber warriors, and while it was not unusual for new tribes to move into old land, these pale men were different because they did not share ways, they imposed theirs. And theirs was a better way that did not demand the silliness of the sacrifice.

But he must not let his people die.

Among the camp of the pales were many tribes that sided with the newcomers against Moctezuma. One man recognized the Actatl king, and he went to the woman of Cortez and said, "That is not a slave but king of the Actatl." And the woman called the king to her and asked why he had come as a slave when as a king he would have been welcome.

"Have you told this to Cortez yet?" asked the king.

"I will tell him before sunrise," said the queen of the coastal people. And with the sharper, harder metal of the pale men, the king slit her throat. He did not take her heart.

When his hands were dry, he went to Cortez and told him of what he had heard as a young slave—that there were cities to the north of Moctezuma's that were of pure gold. The walls were gold. The ceilings were gold. The streets were gold.

Cortez asked why he had not told him this earlier.

"Oh, great lord of the pale men, I was asked by your woman for rooms of gold. In these cities of the north, they do not keep gold in rooms. They make bricks of gold and they build with it, so plentiful is this strange metal."

And with a glorious laugh, Cortez ordered his expedition to prepare. In the excitement the death of one translator, even a coastal queen, was not taken as an undue tragedy. There were many translators now.

Fifteen days north did the king take Cortez and his party and on the fifteenth, while in the mountains, the king slipped away at night.

Losing his guide, Cortez would give up the expedition, but for centuries after, those who followed him would continue to search for the Seven Cities of Cibol, cities that never existed except in the imagination of a king who wished to keep the greedy Spaniards away from him and his people.

13

On that fifteenth night the king left with a horse and one gun with powder and bullets and flint and many books.

And a month later, he arrived at the main city of the Actatl. The king had been gone for four full seasons.

There was a new king now, and the priests of Uctut, in their confusion, announced one king would have to be killed. So the new king, who was a son of the old king, gathered his warriors and prepared to sacrifice his father. But when the first warrior approached, the old king used the thunder stick and, throwing nothing at all, killed the man. All seeing this turned on the new king to make him sacrifice for the old, but the old king would not have this. He had not returned to be king but to bring a message of a new undertaking that Uctut should approve.

The old king would take fifty women and ten young male children and ten young female children, and he would go off with them. But the priests would not have this for that would mean two kings lived and Uctut would be angered.

"Within but a few generations, Uctut will not be," said the old king. "This city will not be. The words we use will not be. The way priest greets king and king priest and people greet their lords will not be. Nothing of the Actatl will be."

They asked if a god had spoken to him in a sacred vision, and so they would understand, he said that Uctut had told him.

This greatly worried the priests, who ordered each family to give a sacrifice so that Uctut would speak to the priests.

14

When the sacrifices were over, a person could not walk on the stone above the well for it sloshed with blood.

Basins of blood filled the cracks and crevices in the steps to the high stone. Red was the well that fed Uctut. Strong was the stench that came from the high stone.

And then there was knowledge. The old king could live, but each who left with him would have to become a priest of Uctut who would have to know the real name of the stone, and should the king's predictions be true, each would have to promise a priest's service to protect Uctut.

In this promise, in a civilization soon to die, in the lush green hills between Mexico and South America, was a seed planted that would sprout more than four hundred years later. Its flower would feed on human life, and nothing in that future world that could put a man on the moon would be able to defend against the descendants of those who still looked upon the shiny yellow moon in the night as another god.

The old king took his new family away toward an uninhabited valley he had seen once on a march. He bred well and he taught well. Each learned language and writing and numbers and the primitive science of the west. And when the new generation of his loins was ready, he sent them out in groups to find the pale invaders—not to kill them for there were too many—but to reproduce with them, taking the best child of each brood and teaching it that it was Actatl. Even if its hair were yellow, still it was Actatl.

For the king had discovered that the only way

15

his people could live was to camouflage themselves in the colors of others, whoever they were.

Only one thing bothered him. He could not break them of Uctut, the silly rock. For while he taught them everything, Uctut and its real name became the one thing even the children knew, but not he. And thus it was prized even more. The more he said it was just a silly rock, the more important Uctut became to them as the symbol of what they had been and what they would preserve in their future lives. So he just stopped talking about it.

One day the last of the original women died, and he realized he was alone. He gave her ritual burial, although piling the stones was hard because he was an old man.

The new village was empty, and the clay tablets upon which Actatl sounds and European speech were written had not been used for many years, since the last trained group of youths had left. The older ones had not taken well to the new language and way of things, and most had stayed with him here in the hidden village. It was empty now, but for an old dog that could hardly move and had cried very much when its master had left years before.

"Done," said the last king of the Actatl. He tried to coax the dog to come with him, but he could not. He put as much food as he could carry into a small bundle and opened the storehouse to the dog, who would probably be a meal for one of the cats of the jungle, now that the man was gone.

The king made the trek back to the city of the

16

Actatl. Even before he set foot there, he knew the kingdom was gone. The roads were grassed over and the fields untilled. Great plants grew in stone watchtowers.

Perhaps a few old friends would be biding their last days, hiding in the remains of the city. But there was no one, not even dogs, left in the great city from which once the empire of the Actatl had been ruled. And something else was strange. There was no sign of the fires that usually accompanied a siege.

He thought, Yes, the Spaniards have been here. All the gold had been removed. But the pieces, he saw, had not been torn away or hacked away or ripped away but were carefully taken out. He thought for a moment, with great happiness, that one of the later kings had wisely taken the people away, something the old king knew he never could get the priests to agree to. But when he arrived at the high stone altar, he knew otherwise, and he let out from his stomach a deep wail. Whitened bones covered the steps and formed in great piles, already mingling with plants. A small tree grew from the mouth of a grinning skull.

He knew what had happened. Hearing of the Spaniards nearby, they had all come to the high place, hiding what they knew would be of value to the pale men invaders. And they had killed themselves here, their last offering to Uctut. Probably one group killing another, until the last made himself sacrifice to Uctut. He noticed the chest bones chipped on the lower bodies, but higher up there was no such bone breakage. Probably the first were sacrificed ritually, and as the days of

17

blood wore on the killing became like the tilling of a field, something to be gotten over with as quickly and effectively as possible. At the top stones he saw skulls with holes in them, and this confirmed his guess. At the end they were smashing in heads.

He was tired, more of spirit than of his old body.

He looked up at the carved rock, a king's height, and said, "Uctut"—for he did not know its secret name—"you are not even stupid because people are stupid and you are not people. You are a rock. A rock made special by people. You are like a pebble that gets in the way of a plow. Rock. Stupid rock."

He sat down, pushing bones aside, amazed at how light they were, now dried, and he was tired. And on the fourth day he felt something sharp at his heart and reached weakly to his chest just to assure himself that there was no blood. There was none, of course, and he shut his eyes and he felt good and wanting of death in a natural way. And he slipped away into that deepest sleep, knowing his job was well done.

Centuries passed, and with nothing special to preserve the bones of all who were there, they blended into the natural substances from which they came. Not even the dreams remained when a heavy rope crane dragged the king-high stone with the carving from the high place. Other men chopped up stones with carvings on them, but this stone would be worth more uncut, even though it took four mules to drag it through the jungles and over the mountains, where men with Aztec

18

faces and Spanish names sold it to the highest bidder.

Uctut, the stone, came to a large museum in New York City on Central Park West and was incorrectly put into a display of Aztec art. One day a German businessman saw it and suggested that it have a room of its own. A wealthy Detroit industrialist made a large contribution to the museum and, on becoming a trustee of that institution, moved to follow the suggestion of the German.

The curator objected, saying it was a rather insignificant piece of pre-Aztec work and didn't deserve a whole room, and shortly thereafter, to his surprise, he was dismissed for his "surly and unprofessional attitude."

A Japanese architect designed the new room for the stone with a rather gross, heavy wall blocking out the north light from what had been a fine window. And the architect even put in a large water fountain, although there was a drinking fountain just outside.

Apparently, the new trustee and architect knew what they were doing because this stone received many visitors from all over the world. A fiery Arab radical visited it on the same day as an Israeli paratroop colonel, and apparently the stone had some sort of soothing effect because they not only seemed to get along, but they embraced just before leaving. Both, when asked if this had happened by their countrymen, denied the incident. Of course, none seemed as enamored of this pre-Aztec stone as Count Ruy Lopez de Goma y Sanches, who came every day.

19

One October evening, a guard discovered that someone with a spray can of green enamel-glow had written in large letters on the stone: "Joey 172."

The next day, the congressman from the district was found in his Washington office with his chest over a pool of blood.

His heart had been ripped out.

Chapter Two

His name was Remo, and he was disbelieving his ears.

"Remo, this is Smith. Get back to Folcroft right away."

"Who's this?" Remo asked.

"Harold W. Smith, your employer."

"I can't hear you. The waves here are too loud," said Remo, looking at the quiet gentle roll of the sea green Atlantic coming onto the white sandy beach of Nag's Head, South Carolina.

The motel room was quiet also but for the faint scratching of goose quill against parchment. A wisp of an aged Oriental worked the quill quickly, yet his long-nailed fingers scarcely seemed to move. He would pause and look off into that well of creativity and write again, hardly moving his golden morning kimono.

"I said you've got to come back to Folcroft right away. Everything is coming apart."

"You said you want to speak to a Harold Smith?" Remo said.

"I know this is an open line but ..." Remo heard buzzing. Someone had cut them off. He put down the receiver.

"I'll be back in a while, Little Father," Remo said, and Chiun turned regally from his scriptures.

"Were you cringing and fat, or were you lying in the dirt when I found you?" asked Chiun. The voice was squeaky and hit highs and lows like a mountain range of slate with giant paws scratching across it.

"Neither," said Remo. "I was coming out of unconsciousness. I was pretty healthy for this civilization. As a matter of fact, I was pretty healthy for almost any time or place. Except one place."

"And lo," intoned Chiun—the quill had become a blur of speed, yet each Korean character of the writing remained clear and precise—"did Chiun, the Master of Sinanju, see the groveling white amid the garbage of his birth. Deformed of limb he was. Dull of eye he was with strange round orbs set in his head. But most deformed, saw the Master of Sinanju, was this white in his mind. A dull, sodden, lifeless mass in his ugly pale skull."

"I thought you had already contributed your section about me to the history of Sinanju," Remo said.

"I am revising it," Chiun said.

"I'm glad I see you writing this because now, with great certainty, I can reject the whole history of your village as bilge and fantasy and nonsense. Remember I've seen the village of Sinanju. We have better-looking sewer systems in this country."

"Like all whites and blacks, you are prejudiced," said Chiun, and his voice became scriptural again. "And, lo, the Master of Sinanju said unto this wretch, 'Arise, I shall make you whole. You shall know your senses and your mind. You shall breathe clean air fully in your whole body. You shall have life in you as no white has ever had.' And the wretch knew that grace was upon him, and he said, 'Oh, Awesome Magnificence, why do you bestow such gracious gifts upon one as low as I?' "

"Blow it out your ears," Remo said. "I've got work. I'll be back soon."

Late summer in Nag's Head, South Carolina, had all the charm of a roaster bag in an overheated oven. Remo saw car windows rolled up with people preserved by air conditioning. Those who were on the street this steamy day lagged as if their feet were weighted with lead.

Remo moved briskly. He was just short of six feet and thin but for the extra thickness in his wrists. He had sharp features and high cheekbones that seemed a platform for dark penetrating eyes that some women had told him made their stomachs "liquidy."

"Hey, don't you sweat?" asked the clerk as Remo stepped into a small luncheonette and asked for change.

"Only when it's hot," said Remo.

"It's a hundred and five outside," said the clerk.

"Then I'm sorry, I forgot to," Remo said. Actually he knew that sweating was only one form of cooling the overheated body and not the most efficient form. Breathing was, but most people did not know how to breathe, treating it like some function that had to be looked after only when you noticed it wasn't working right. From proper breathing came the rhythms of life and power.

"Funny, ah ain't ever seen nobody not sweat on a day liken today, not even a nigra," said the clerk. "How you do it?"

Remo shrugged. "You wouldn't understand if I told you, anyhow."

"You think ah'm dumb. You some smart yankee, come down hyeah, think ah'm dumb."

"Not until you opened your mouth," said Remo and went to the telephone booth. He piled up the change in front of him. He dialed the 800-area code emergency feed number. It was designed more for availability than security, but he could always leave a message for the real Harold W. Smith to call him back at the phone booth.

"I am sorry sir," came the distant voice of a tape recording. "The number you have reached is not in service at this time. If you need assistance, please wait and an operator will be with you in a moment."

Remo hung up and dialed again and got the same message again. This time he waited. A live operator answered with a nonregional sort of voice—neither the guttural consonants of the northeast, the syrup of the south, or the twang of the midwest. California, thought Remo. The drop phone number is in California.

"Can I help you?"

"Yes," said Remo. And he gave the number he had tried to dial.

"You're where, now?" asked the operator.

"Chillicothe, Ohio," lied Remo. "Why is that number not working?"

"Because, according to our records, this number has never worked. You're not in Chillicothe."

"Thank you," said Remo.

"But we do have some information on this number." And she gave him another number, and this was even stranger because if Smith had set this up, he would never have given out an alternate number. And it occurred to Remo that the operator was not there to give him information but to find out where he was. He hung up.

Outside a gray and white police car with a red bubble atop parked at the curb. Two heavy officers with hands on pistols were out of the car lumbering into the luncheonette. The clerk ducked. Remo left the booth.

"Were you in that booth making a telephone call?" asked the first officer. The other moved to one side so Remo would be facing two guns.

"No," said Remo.

"Who was in that booth then?"

"How should I know?" Remo said.

"He was in that booth," said the clerk from behind the counter. "He's a weirdo, Jethro. Watch him. He don't sweat."

"I want to talk to you," said the officer.

25

"You seem to be accomplishing that," said Remo.

"Down at headquarters," said the officer.

"Are you arresting me or what?"

"Just to talk. People want to talk to you."

"Weirdo don't sweat, Jethro," said the clerk rising from behind the counter.

"Shut up, Luke," said the officer.

"I do too sweat," said Remo. "That's slander."

And when they were in the air conditioned offices of the Nag's Head Police Department, Remo perspired while others complained of the chill. Two men who said they were lawyers from a joint congressional committee investigating CIA and FBI abuses arrived and said they wanted to talk to Remo. They wore three-hundred-dollar suits and didn't comb their hair. Remo was not being charged with anything, but he had phoned a telephone number they were interested in, they said. This number had come to light on an FBI voucher no one could explain. Perhaps Remo could help. Why did he phone that number, who gave it to him, what was it used for?

"I can't believe this," Remo said. "You guys have come all this way to check some guy's expense account phone calls?"

"It's not exactly just a phone number. We have discovered that within the FBI and CIA there were whole units unaccounted for in their investigative work. Incomplete files on American citizens that seemed to lead nowhere and a loose tie-in to a computer system that the committee investigators could not locate," said one of the lawyers.

"That makes you pretty important, fella," the other lawyer told Remo.

"We've had our own experts check out leads into this system and they believe it is massive. Massive," said the first lawyer.

"That makes you very, very important," said the second lawyer.

"So do yourself a favor, fella, and tell us why you were dialing that number, and maybe we can do you a favor."

Remo stopped perspiring. He had to leave soon. He had promised Chiun he would be back quickly.

"Like what?" he said. "Not charging me with felonious dialing? Conspiracy to make a phone call? Aiding and abetting the Bell System?"

"How about material witness in a murder, fella? How about material witness, if not suspect, in the murder of a United States congressman investigating coverup operations? How does that thrill ya, fella?"

"Because I tried to make a phone call, I'm a murder suspect?"

"Because you tried to reach that phone number, fella. Now we know that number appeared on an FBI voucher no one seems to know about. We know that in the last three months of the investigation, only one person has called that number. You. We know there was a congressman looking into that computer network and intelligence money hidden in federal budgets. And we know that he's dead now with his heart ripped out of his body. It's not just any phone number anymore, fella."

"It's a gazelle?" asked Remo innocently.

27

"You know we can hold you as a material witness," said the second lawyer.

"Feel free," said Remo, and he gave the cover name and address, which was proper procedure for arrest. When this name and address was forwarded to FBI files to check for any previous arrests—a routine police function—the FBI clerk would find a forwarding number listed on it, and within twenty minutes the computers at Folcroft Sanitarium would spin out orders to another government agency to get Remo released officially from wherever he was being held in the United States.

The whole process, Smith had assured him, would take no more than two hours, possibly three if the jail were relatively inaccessible. The fingerprints, of course, would check with nothing in the vast FBI files. Not with a service record, a security clearance, or an arrest, because they had been permanently disposed of by the FBI itself more than a decade ago. They did not keep fingerprints of dead men.

So when Remo was told he had his last chance to shed some light on the telephone number he had dialed from the luncheonette in Nag's Head or the horror killing of the congressman who had been investigating covert government operations, Remo said they could throw away the key if they liked.

The cell was small with fresh gray painted iron bars set into the normal flat iron frame that locked by pushing a steel stud, click, into a receiver socket. It looked formidable if you did not understand it in the Sinanju way.

28

Remo sat down on the hard cot suspended from the wall and remembered the last cell he had been in more than a decade before.

He had been waiting for death then when a monk entered his cell to give him last rites and told him to swallow a pill at the end of the crucifix, right at the moment he was strapped into the electric chair. He did and passed out, and when he recovered there were burns on his arms and ankles, and the first people he'd found yet who believed he had not committed a murder were talking to him. They believed that because they had framed him, a neat plan by Harold W. Smith, director of CURE.

"Never heard of it," Remo had said and the lemony-faced Smith allowed that if Remo had heard of it, the country as they knew it would be finished. CURE had been set up because regular government agencies could not deal effectively with growing chaos within the constitution. CURE provided the extralegal help the country needed to survive. It lacked only one thing—a killer arm. Remo was it, the man who didn't exist for the organization that didn't exist. As one who had just been electrocuted, he was a nonperson. Dead men had no fingerprints.

At first Remo had thought he would just escape at the first opportunity. But one mission led to another, and then there was the training with Chiun, through which he really became someone else, and each day the person he had been before he was electrocuted died a little bit more. And he stayed on the job.

Now, more than a decade later, Remo Williams

waited in the southern jail cell for the computers at Folcroft Sanitarium, CURE's nerve center, to spin off their untraceable orders for his release. Two hours, three at the most.

So he waited. Two hours, three hours, four hours, as the water dripped into the sink and a lone fly made its erratic energized way up the cell block and down toward a fan that spun slowly enough to keep the air placid, hot, and steamy. Humidity droplets formed on the slick gray paint of the bars, and a drunk in the next cell with body odor pungent enough to rust aluminum began philosophizing about life.

"Enough," said Remo and joined two fingers of his left hand on top of the square metal lock. He felt the warm wetness of the slick paint against the skin grooves of his fingers. Beginning ever so lightly, for the rhythm of the pressure was the key to this move, he lowered the skin of the paint downwards, crushing the thin layer of rust underneath. More pressure and the frame strained at its hinges. The fly lit on a bar and popped off as if stung by electricity. A bolt of the bar frame lost a thread with a crack, and then the lock snapped with a dull snap like a piece of lead falling on a stack of mimeograph paper. Remo pushed the door open and it squealed off its bottom hinge.

"Sumbitch," yelled the drunk foggily. "They don't make 'em the way they used to. Can you open mine?"

And with two fingers pressing just on the lock, Remo released the second cell door. The drunk rolled his feet off the cot to the floor, and seeing he would have to take at least three steps to get out of his cell, decided to escape later. He thanked the generous stranger and passed out.

A guard poked his head into the corridor and, realizing what had happened, slammed the iron corridor door. He was bolting it when it slammed right back at him as if a jet plane were coming through it. Remo walked over him and down a long approach corridor until he found a door. It led to the police station. A detective looked up, startled.

"I didn't like the accommodations," said Remo and was off, down another corridor before the detective could get his gun out. He slowed to a casual walk, asked an officer filling out a form where the exit was, and was out of the building by the time someone shouted: "Prisoner escaped."

Nag's Head was not the sort of town in which one could get lost in a crowd, so Remo chose backyards and high palmettos, becoming one with the green and sandy landscape under the blood red sun of the late afternoon.

At the motel, Chiun was gazing at the Atlantic churning custard tops of foam as it came into the long white sandy beach, spread out flat, then slipped back into itself again, to come back in another green and white wave.

"We've got to run," said Remo.

"From whom?" Chiun asked, astonished.

"The local police. We've got to get back to Folcroft."

"Run from police? Does not Emperor Smith rule the police?"

"Not exactly. It's sort of complicated."

31

"What is he emperor of then?"

"The organization," Remo said.

"And the organization has no influence with the police?"

"Yes and no. Especially not now. I think he's in trouble."

"He reminds me of a Caliph of Samarkand who was so afraid to show weakness he would not even confide in his assassin, who was, of course, at that time a Master of Sinanju. When fortune turned against this Caliph, the Master was unable to help him. So too with Emperor Smith. We have done what we could do and we can help him no longer."

"He's in deep trouble."

"Because he did not confide in you," Chiun said, "and therefore it is not our responsibility. You have done everything you could for this silly man and now you must take your talents where they are properly honored. I have always thought that Sinanju was a waste for this man."

"As there are some things you cannot get me to understand, Little Father," Remo said, thoughtfully, "so too are there things that I cannot explain to you."

"That's because you are stupid, Remo. I am not stupid."

Remo looked at the large lacquered steamer trunks.

"We won't have time for those. We'll have to get them later."

"I am not leaving my meager possessions to go looking for an unworthy emperor who has not trusted the House of Sinanju."

"I'm sorry," Remo said. "I'll have to go my-self."

"You would abandon a gentle aging man in the twilight of his golden years?"

"What twilight? What golden? What gentle?" asked Remo. "You're the deadliest assassin on earth."

"I provide honest service for honest proper tribute," said Chiun.

"Goodbye," said Remo. "See you later."

Chiun turned away.

Chapter Three

Undoubtedly there would be roadblocks and a statewide search for him, so Remo decided to use a passing tractor trailer until he was out of South Carolina.

He rode in between new Chromacolor televisions and automatic defrost refrigerators in the back of the trailer, black as a cave. He could not hear the driver in the motor cabin up front, and the driver had not heard him enter. Once out of the state there was little chance he would even be stopped. To a saddeningly large degree the only way fugitives got caught nowadays was if they told someone who they were and where they were, or if they were collared committing a major felony, and their fingerprints were checked out properly with FBI files in Washington.

Once in North Carolina, there would be no worry.

Remo listened to the crates of appliances straining against their metal strappings. Something was wrong with the organization, terminally wrong, if it could not even get him out of a little jail cell.

That first frantic phone call over an open line to his motel room, that really had been Smitty's voice, and that was something Smitty never would do unless all his other channels had fouled up.

Maybe it was better anyway that the organization was coming apart. What had it done? Put a temporary crimp in a landslide that was taking the country with it anyhow? Maybe you couldn't change history. As Chiun had so often said: "Your greatest strength is knowing what you cannot do."

When the truck stopped and Remo heard two drivers get out talking about food, he slipped from the trailer and saw he was in the outskirts of a large city.

It was night and the offensive odor of greasy meat frying felt like it came from an aerosol can. He was near a large diner, and as he stopped a cab was just pulling out. The painted sign on the side of the taxi said, Raleigh, North Carolina.

"Airport," said Remo, and within twenty minutes he was at the small Raleigh-Durham airport and within an hour on a Piedmont Airlines flight to New York City, where he rented a car at

LaGuardia, and by three A.M. he was approaching the high stone walls of Folcroft Sanitarium in Rye, New York.

The one-way windows of Smith's office overlooking Long Island Sound seemed like dull yellow squares in the early morning blackness. The lights were on. No guard stopped him at the gate. The door to the main building was open. Remo skipped up a flight of darkened stairs and down a corridor to a large wooden door. Even in the darkness, he could see the staid gold lettering:

"Dr. Harold W. Smith, Director."

The door was unlocked. It led to a room of desks where Smith's secretaries worked during the day. Remo heard a familiar high-pitched voice come from Smith's inner office. It vowed eternal support in these times of trouble. It lauded Emperor Smith for his wisdom, courage, and generosity. It promised a bloodbath for his enemies.

It was Chiun.

"How'd you get here so fast?" asked Remo in Korean. Chiun's long fingernails stopped in the midst of an eloquent gesture. Smith sat behind the large, well-polished desk, his dry face precisely shaved. He wore a dark suit with vest and a fresh tie and a spotless white shirt.

Three A.M. The man was facing an obvious disaster and he looked as if he had only paused for a coffee break in a Wall Street office. He must have been the only baby ever to toilet train himself in the first week of life. Remo never remembered seeing Smith without a crease in his pants.

"It is of no importance how I got here. I must

extricate you from this idiot emperor and his disaster," Chiun answered in Korean.

"What about your trunks?"

"I have more invested in you. Ten arduous years without so much as a mite of repayment for the great gifts of knowledge I have bestowed upon you. I will not let you just run off with my investment."

"If I may interrupt," said Smith, "I think we have important business. I don't understand Korean."

"Neither does Remo, really," said Chiun in English. "But it is our thing to know things to serve you better."

"Thank you," said Smith. "Remo, I have what may be shocking news to you. We're not only just in trouble but I've had to—"

"Shut down most of the systems," Remo interrupted.

"Let him finish," scolded Chiun.

"Shut down most of the systems," said Smith.

"You see," said Chiun to Remo. "Now you know."

"We're virtually inoperative," Smith continued. "We could have survived those ignorant investigations of the CIA and FBI where we have linked systems that they don't know about. But after that gruesome insanity with the congressman, they started looking all over and they stumbled onto a few of our systems. I phoned you direct, hoping you wouldn't rely on one of our special phone numbers."

"I did."

"Lucky you didn't get picked up."

"I did," said Remo.

"Kill anyone?"

"Of course," said Chiun.

"No," said Remo.

"Good," said Smith.

"Of course not," said Chiun. "Peaceful as a monk. Awaiting only your word to slay your enemies."

"I'm afraid that just eliminating someone won't do here," Smith said. "It won't relieve the pressure on us. You've got to find out who or what did that killing of the congressman and then make it clear to the world. Have it or them confess or be convicted. That should take the pressure off this investigation."

"Are there any leads?"

"None," said Smith. "The congressman's heart was ripped out. And they didn't even find it."

"By hand?" asked Remo.

"Not exactly, as far as we could tell. It appeared like some very crude knife."

"No trace of the heart?"

"None."

"Sounds like some lover's quarrel," Remo said.

"Man didn't have a love life. He was married," Smith said, thinking of his own thirty-year marriage. "A normal happy marriage that just grinds on and on."

"Like the incessant dropping of water," said Chiun.

"Yes. Something like that," Smith said.

"I had one of those once," Chiun said, "but one day she slipped on a rock near the windy bay and

38

drowned. So you see, patience makes all things turn out well."

"In any case," Smith said, "this congressman was clean. He didn't have any but political enemies. He was safely guarded, they thought. The man assigned to him by the Justice Department when this investigation started was outside his office door all night. He got suspicious at about five A.M., and when he checked, he found the congressman slumped over his desk. His shirt had been unbuttoned and the heart was out. Arteries and valves severed. Incredible amount of blood."

"Amateurs," said Chiun disdainfully. "The first sign is sloppiness."

"So you have to be careful," Smith said. "The FBI and the CIA are just as anxious as we are to get the right man. The only problem is that they think it may be us, some secret organization that they don't know anything about. If they suspect you're with our organization, they might just scoop you up."

"I'll be careful," Remo said.

"I'm going to start closing this place down for a while," Smith said. "The computers have been washed clean already, and most of the staff has been cut loose. In a few days there won't be a trace. Everything else is up to you."

"Okay," said Remo.

"More than okay," said Chiun. "We shall find this menace and destroy it."

"Not destroy," said Smith, clearing his throat. "Identify and have him publicly convicted. This is not an assassination."

"But of course," said Chiun. "Your wisdom is
39

beyond that of a simple assassin. You are truly an emperor, most formidable."

Outside in the cooler night with the salt wind coming in off the Long Island Sound, Chiun said in Korean to Remo:

"I have always said that Smith is a lunatic, and tonight he has proved it."

And this reminded him of a czar who, when he went insane, asked the court assassin to clean the stables. "That one wanted a stable cleaner, and this one wants I do not know what."

"He wants someone convicted," Remo said.

"Oh. A representative of justice, a speaker in the courts of law. A lawyer. I would rather clean stables."

"Not exactly," said Remo. "We've got to find out who and then get the evidence to some prosecutor."

"Oh, like soldiers, policemen, and detectives do?" asked Chiun.

"Sort of."

"I see," said Chiun. "We are looking for some one or something, but we are not exactly sure what or who, and we are not exactly sure what we are supposed to do to this someone or something, but we do know that if we don't succeed in what we do not know, Emperor Smith will suffer."

"I know what I'm doing," Remo said. "Don't worry."

"Worry?" said the latest Master of Sinanju. "One would have to stop laughing to worry. You whites are so funny."

40

Chapter Four

Mrs. Ramona Harvey Delpheen was examining a chart of bicentennial celebrations when a long yellow feather fell over a blue outlined box called "Columbus Circle Monument Parade." She looked up.

Mrs. Delpheen was a portly woman whose flesh had been pampered by expensive oils and skilled fingers so that when she smiled it looked as if delicate creases had jumped from hiding. She smiled intensely because she was surprised by these men and also they looked rather funny.

"What are you fellows doing in all those feathers?" she said, laughing. She thought she recognized one, a rather untalented lad who somehow had gotten control of a publishing company.

Met him at a party or somewhere. The other men were strangers, and she was not quite sure why the butler had let them through the main door of her Fifth Avenue residence without announcing them first. There was so much trouble nowadays on the New York City streets outside that one should never allow strangers access to the house proper. She was sure that she had made this very clear to the butler.

"We already have a group of Indians for the Columbus Circle affair," said Mrs. Delpheen. "Besides, it's an Italian-American day," she added.

The men said nothing. The long robes of yellow feathers hung down to their knees and were open in front, revealing bare chests and white loin cloths.

"I said we already have a very fine band of Mohawk dancers. Those aren't even American Indian trappings you're wearing. More South American, if you will. Aztec."

"Not Aztec," said the farthest man, who held what appeared to be a phallic symbol made of a light colored chipped stone. The other four men stood at the sides like a formation of twos.

"Well, we can't use Mayas either," she said.

"Not Maya."

"You don't look like Indians anyway," said Mrs. Delpheen, forcing the smile now. She fingered a pearl at the end of a strand that hung looping over her ample breasts enclosed in basic black. The pearls became sweat-slippery in her hands.

"We are all of Indian blood," said the man with the pointed stone.

"That's lovely," said Mrs. Delpheen. "I think the beauty of America is that so many groups have made such significant contributions. But you see, the . . . uh . . . Incas weren't one of them."

"Not Inca. Actatl."

"I've never heard of them."

"Because you would not allow us to live. Not in our real skins. So we chose your skins and your hair and your eyes, but we are all Actatl. All we wished for was to live. But you would not let us. Not in our real skins. Now you have violated what we hold precious and worthy, the stone of our ancestors, the life force of our hearts, the most gracious and central inspiration of our being. So holy that you may only know it as Uctut."

"Well, I'm certainly sorry for anything I have done. I'm sure we can make amends."

"You shall."

Two of the men in feathered capes latched onto Mrs. Delpheen's wrists, and she said there was no need to be physical. But when the other two reached for her ankles, she had another idea.

"All right, if it's kinky rape you want, I can't stop you. But at least let's go into the bedroom."

They hoisted her bulky frame to the desk top, and the man with the pointed stone chanted a monotone song in a language and tune she did not recognize. She tried twisting an arm from a locking grip, but it only was gripped even more firmly. She tried kicking, but she couldn't get a leg back far enough for a good forward thrust. She smelled the sharp odor of fear and excitement, like urine mixed with a stale perfume. The

43

man holding her right wrist had pupil-wide eyes, just like her first husband had had at orgasm. Sweat made his yellowish forehead glisten in the gentle light from the crystal cut chandelier overhead. A small stone replica of an Egyptian pyramid she had used for a paperweight cut painfully into her right hip, but she could not get her body shifted to avoid it. The two men at her ankles joined their free hands, pinning her belly also.

Looking up at the chandelier, she had a strange thought. It had not been dusted for a long while, and that was all she could think of. The chandelier had not been dusted, and probably the one in the main hall was the same.

Both of the men holding at her hands simultaneously reached to her neck and with a single rip tore down the top of her basic black dress. They also unleashed the pearls which clicked across the desk top and fell chattering to the wood parquet floor. Then one unsnapped her bra.

"Talk about kinky," said Mrs. Delpheen. "Do you fellows need feathers to get it up?"

The man with the phallic symbol of stone raised it above her head, and to Mrs. Delpheen, her dress half-off down to her waist, the downward thrust of the stone seemed very slow until it rammed into her chest. Not cut, rammed. Like someone had hit her chest with a ball peen hammer that kept going inside, and then she saw very clearly the stone move slowly toward her navel, and it felt like pulleys were ripping her insides out, taking her shoulders into her body, and then she screamed—a wail stifled by a lack of air coming into her. She saw a big grin on the face of the fifth man, pulling the stone around her chest.

"More," he said. "Scream more."

And then the chandeliers didn't matter any more because they were now away, going far away down a long tunnel that became gray, then black, and quickly nothing to worry about any more.

The man with the stone knife saw the fat face become flat and almost waxy, and he knew there would be no more screams of honor to Uctut. He worked quickly, severing the last arteries, and then with a rip he tore the heart out of the body cavity and held it aloft, still pumping bloodily in his hands. There was no need for the two at the arms to hold on any longer, and they reached behind them under their robes where leather thongs held clay bowls.

Each unsnapped his bowl and waited while the heart pumped violently and then with a small flutter stopped. The man with the stone knife delicately placed the mass of bloody muscle into one upturned bowl. The second bowl went on top with a neat interlocking click.

The men at the ankles turned the lifeless hulk over so that the open chest cavity faced downward over the desk. And the man who had cut out the heart left a typewritten note with its corners carefully smeared with Mrs. Delpheen's blood.

Remo heard about the killing in New York City just as he and Chiun entered Dulles Airport outside Washington. They had gone there, Remo had

45

said, to examine "the scene of the crime" where the congressman had been killed.

"What crime?" Chiun had asked. "Smith said nothing of robbery or deceit, or worse, not paying a worker for his just efforts."

"The killing," Remo had said. "That's what crime."

"Was it not paid for?" Chiun asked.

"The killing was the crime," Remo had said.

"Then every leader of every country is a criminal. No, this is impossible. Emperors cannot be criminals because they make the laws. Those who defy emperors are criminals."

"It's against the law in this country to kill someone," Remo had said.

Chiun had thought a moment, then shook his head.

"Impossible. That would make us criminals, and we most certainly are not. A criminal is someone without our strong standards."

"It's complicated," Remo said. "Take my word for it. It's complicated."

"I do not need your word for it," Chiun had said, and he told a banker from Des Moines, sitting across the aisle from them, that the American way of life was incredibly inscrutable, but if it worked to America's satisfaction, Chiun was not one to complain.

That had been in the plane. Now in the airport Remo heard a pocket radio news report and caught the last words about the second such killing. The afternoon *Washington Star* had a small story:

New York (API)—A rich widow was discovered slain in her fashionable home here today in a manner similar to that of the congressman investigating legal abuses by the FBI and CIA. The woman, Mrs. Ramona H. Delpheen, 51, was found by her butler, slumped over her desk, her heart ripped from her body.

Remo paid for the newspaper but returned it to its stack.

"Well," said Chiun, "I await your brilliant plan to go looking for someone, you do not know who, to do something to him, you do not know what, in a place where he may or may not be, but was once."

"I've changed my mind," Remo said, somewhat embarrassed.

"How can you change what you have yet to show?" Chiun asked.

"We're going to New York."

"I like New York," said Chiun. "It has some restaurants that aren't foreign. Of course, the Korean restaurants are not the best, but very good considering how far they are from civilization."

The shuttle flight to New York took less than an hour, the cab ride from the airport twice that.

Chiun made a small comment that they had gone to four cities so far, and perhaps they might try Tacoma. He had not discovered Tacoma, Washington, yet. Remo said Chiun could go back and watch his trunks if he wished. Chiun said there was nothing worth more than seeing what Remo planned to do next. Perhaps he would like to clean a stable.

47

A uniformed patrolman stood in front of the Delpheen mansion. Remo walked by him with authority. Chiun stopped to chat. He asked the patrolman what he was doing there. The patrolman said there had been a murder committed there the night before. Chiun asked why the patrolman hadn't been there the night before instead.

He did not wait for an answer. The door opened for Remo. A gaunt man in a white jacket and dark pants refused Remo entrance. Chiun muttered in Korean how foolish it was to use doors that were closed to you when the windows in the upper floors were of such easy access and were always open to you. But, he added, the people who used windows usually knew what they were looking for.

"The family is not receiving visitors," said the butler.

"I'm not exactly a visitor," said Remo, sidestepping past the butler. As the butler turned to stop Remo, Chiun went by the other side.

"Where'd the killing take place?" Remo asked.

"I must ask you to leave," the butler said.

"We'll be going in a minute. Relax," Remo said.

"Miss Delpheen is in a deep state of shock, over grief for her mother. You must leave."

A young woman, her gray blue eyes staring dumbly into a far-off nowhere, padded into the main hall. She wore white shorts and a white blouse, and her small anklet sneakers moved sluggishly. A tennis racket hung limply from her right hand. She had sandy yellow hair and her skin was gently golden from much sun.

"I can't believe it," she said softly. "I can't believe it."

"I'm sorry to hear about your mother," Remo said. "She was your mother, wasn't she?"

"Who?" said the girl, pausing under a large chandelier that looked like an upside-down bush of glass.

"The tragedy. The woman who was killed."

"Oh. Mother. Yes. She's dead. I can't believe it."

"I've come to help," Remo said.

"I can't believe it," the girl repeated. "Six-four, six-two, six-love. And I double faulted four times. I never double fault. Once, maybe, if I'm on the verge of death."

"Tennis?" said Remo. "You're worried about a tennis loss?"

"Loss? It was a fucking massacre. I'm Bobbi Delpheen. What can I do for you?"

"I think you're involved in something far more sinister than you realize. I've come about your mother's death. I've come to help you."

"Mother's taken care of. She's at the morgue. Funeral's been taken care of too. Six-four, six-two, six-love. And I double faulted four times. Four times. Can you believe it?"

"Miss Delpheen," said Remo somberly. "Your mother's been murdered. I don't think the police can help, but I can."

"With what?" she said. She had a perky charm and a sweet face, as though she'd been designed by a cartoonist for a toothpaste company. Cute, thought Remo. White, thought Chiun.

"With your mother's tragedy," Remo said.

49

"Her problems are over. I've got my own. Leave me alone. Four double faults." She shook her head and turned away but Chiun spoke up.

"I can teach you to never twice error," he said, looking disdainfully at Remo. For, as he had often said, "To tell the truth to a fool is to be more the fool yourself."

"Double fault," corrected Bobbi Delpheen.

"Yes, that," said Chiun.

"You don't even know how to say it," she said.

"I did not say I would teach you to talk the game, but to play the game. All games of physical skill are the same."

"Tennis isn't like any other game."

"It is like all games. The winners are those who do not let their ignorance defeat them."

"I've been through twenty-eight professional instructors. I don't need some gook philosophy," said Bobbi.

"That instrument hits something, yes," said Chiun, motioning to her steel-framed racket.

"Get these two out of here," said Bobbi Delpheen to the butler.

Chiun's long fingers flickered in the shimmering light of the chandelier. The racket was out of Bobbi's hands and in his, leaving her groping at air. With no more than a gentle slow wrist action, Chiun waved the racket, and then gliding upward in a small leap, knocked crystal pieces from the chandelier above, like harvesting shiny berries from a tree. He was on the floor before the shiny glass pieces reached his open hand. Then, one by one, with a stinging whip of the racket, he hit each crystal down the long hall into the back of a chair. Seven crystals made a single hole the diameter of an espresso cup in the back of a brocaded chair. A tuft of white down sprouted from the small hole.

"I notice you didn't shift weight, didn't drive into the shot," said Bobbi.

"I've come to help," said Remo.

"Shut up," said Bobbi.

"I'll remove them now," said the butler.

"Shut up," said Bobbi.

"Forget the nonsense you have learned," said Chiun. "Your feet do not hit. This instrument hits. I will teach you all, but first you must help me."

"Name it."

"Do as my pupil asks," said Chiun.

"What does he want?" Bobbi asked.

"I could not explain," Chiun said, "for I do not think he knows."

The first place Remo examined was Mrs. Delpheen's study. Chiun watched Remo. Bobbi slumped in a chair, drumming her fingers, bored.

"This is where your mother was killed then?" Remo asked.

"Yes, yes," said Bobbi and blew some air from her puffing cheeks. "The cops say nothing should be touched for a while."

The blood on the desk and floor had dried. And Remo noticed a clot covering a small pointed-up object. He lifted it up, breaking the brownish film around it. A pyramid paperweight. And an outline of its base had been pressed into the hard wood desk. Perhaps someone had leaned on it or had been held down on it. He noticed a bright yellow

51

quill in an inkwell behind the desk. The room was sedate in brown polished wood, dark frames, and dark upholstery, yet the feather of this quill was bright yellow. He lifted it and saw it had no point.

"Was this feather here before your mother was killed?" Remo asked.

"I don't know. This was her study. I never went in," said Bobbi. She made a tennis stroking motion with her right arm, looking at Chiun.

"Later," he said.

"I want to talk to the police and see the body," Remo said.

A homicide lieutenant met the grieving daughter, Bobbi Delpheen, and her two friends at the city morgue, which looked like a gigantic white hospital room with large stainless steel files along one side.

"Look," said the homicide lieutenant, a cigar pegged in the center of his teeth, unlit and oozy. "I'm going out of my way for you people. But I need some cooperation, too. Now, miss, I hope you're sufficiently recovered to answer some of my questions."

Bobbi looked to Remo, who nodded.

"We don't think this was personally motivated, Miss Delpheen, but could you think of anyone who had any ill feeling toward your mother? Who just might want to kill her?" asked the lieutenant.

"Anyone who knew her intimately," said Bobbi. She made another tennis motion with her right hand. Chiun signaled—"later."

"Would that include you?" asked the detective.

"No. I say anyone who knew her intimately.

That would leave me out, and Mother's five husbands, too."

"She was a cold person then?"

"Only to relatives. To everyone else she was hostile and haughty."

"Was your mother engaged in any special activities that you know of?"

"Pick any six. She was a joiner. She was on more committees than that congressman who got it."

"We've already found one that overlapped," said the detective. "They were both on the monuments committee at the museum. Does that mean anything to you?"

"No," said Bobbi, and Chiun had to signal her again that tennis would be later.

"Do you think you're strong enough to view the remains? We're going to have an autopsy tomorrow."

"I thought her heart was ripped out," said Bobbi. "Who needs an autopsy? That probably killed her."

"It was a homicide. This is routine."

The lieutenant pulled back a stainless steel square that looked like a file. It was a morgue slab. A white sheet, dotted with drops of ·brown, covered a series of rises like miniature Wyoming foothills.

"Brace yourselves," said the lieutenant, then he pulled back the sheet. Mrs. Delpheen's face was a frozen, waxy twist of flesh. The mouth was locked open, but the wrinkles, well hidden in life, now streaked down her face, obvious. Her aging breasts hung like melted marshmallows in loose cellophane sacks. And where the middle of her chest had been was now a dark coagulated hole.

"We believe some sort of dull knife and forceps were used," said the detective. "That's what careful scientific analysis told us about the congressman. And the FBI spared no avenue of investigation. Even brought in heart specialists and surgeons."

"What are forceps?" asked Chiun softly.

"They're things you grab with, like pliers," said the detective. Chiun shook his head precisely once. The wisp of beard created a floating wave within itself, then quieted.

"No," said Chiun. "They are wrong. This wound was made by a stone knife."

"How the hell can you tell that?" said the detective disbelievingly.

"Because I look," said Chiun. "If you look, you will see no long tear of murder, which is what happens when the body is torn apart in anger. No. There are small horizontal tears across the arteries, and these are made by a stone knife. Have you ever made a stone knife?"

The detective allowed as he had not.

"A stone knife," said Chiun, "is made by chipping to sharp edges, not grinding straight like metal. And these sorts of knives are sharp at some points and not sharp at others. They are used more like saws after they go into something. Do you see?"

"No kidding?" said the detective. A cold ash fell from his unlit cigar into the chest cavity as he peered into the body. "Sorry," he said. The detective puzzled a moment.

54

"Maybe you can help us with something else," he said. From the left breast pocket in his shiny seersucker jacket he took a photocopy sheet rolled up like a scroll.

It was about eight inches wide but twenty-four inches long and had twelve dark sections of writing when it was unrolled.

"What's this?" asked the detective, handing the sheet to Chiun. "We made it from an original found under the head of the body."

Chiun looked at the long sheet carefully. He examined the edges. He felt the surface of the paper, then nodded wisely.

"This is a copy of a document produced by an American machine that makes such copies."

"Yeah, we know it's a photocopy, but what does the note mean?"

"It is in twelve different languages," said Chiun. "And one of them I do not understand, nor have I seen. The Chinese I know, the French and Arabic I know, the Hebrew and Russian I know. Here it is again, in real language. In Korean. The Sanskrit and Aramaic I know. The Swahili and the Urdu and Spanish I know. But the first language I do not know."

"We think it's a ritual murder and the note is part of the ritual. Death for kicks sort of thing," said the detective. Remo glanced over Chiun's shoulders at the note.

"What do you think, Remo?" asked Chiun.

"Is he an expert?" asked the detective.

"He is learning," said Chiun.

"I don't know," said Remo, "but I'd guess all those languages say the same thing."

Chiun nodded.

"But what is this symbol here?" Remo pointed to a rough rectangular drawing in the middle of the text of the unknown language.

"In the other languages on this paper, it is called an Uctut," said Chiun.

"What is an Uctut?" asked Remo.

"I do not know. What is a Joey 172?" Chiun asked.

"I don't know. Why?" said Remo.

"Because that is in the note, too," Chiun said.

"So what does it all mean?" asked the detective. "We've had trouble making heads or tails out of it."

Chiun raised his delicate hands and signaled ignorance.

Outside, in the muggy, grimy New York City streets, with traffic jammed to a horn-blaring standstill, Chiun explained.

"It was a note of demand for reparations," he said. "It was not clear because it was written in the lofty language of a religion. But whoever wrote it demands that a 'Joey 172' be punished for some sort of offense to an Uctut. And until this country punishes this Joey 172, then the servants of Uctut will continue to ease his pain with blood."

"I still don't understand," said Remo.

"Your country gives up Joey 172, whatever that is, or more will die," said Chiun.

"Who gives a shit?" asked Bobbi.

"I do," said Remo.

"This bright, beautiful, and charming young woman makes much sense," said Chiun.

"If you care, then do your thing," Bobbi said to Remo. "Find Joey 172."

"She makes sense," Chiun said, "when she is not talking stupid. Like now."

Remo smiled. "I think I know how to find Joey 172. Have you ever ridden on a New York City subway?"

"No," said Chiun, and he was not about to.

Chapter Five

Antwan Pedaster Jackson felt he had an obliga-
tion to bring wisdom to whites. For example, the
old woman with the frayed brown shopping bag
riding on the rear of the "D" train after seven
P.M. Didn't she know that whites weren't supposed to ride the subways after that hour? She
sure enough seemed to realize it now as he
moseyed into the empty car with Sugar Baby
Williams, both seniors at Martin Luther King
High School, where Sugar Baby was going to
graduate as valedictorian because he could read
faster than anyone else and without moving his
lips either, except on the hard words. But even
the teacher couldn't read the hard words at Martin Luther King.

"You know where you is?" asked Antwan.

The old woman, her face lined with years of toil, looked up from her rosary, fingering a Hail Mary. A faded yellow and red babushka cradled her heartlike face. She moved the paper shopping bag tighter between her knees.

"I am sorry I do not speak the English well," she said.

"This the Noo Yawk subway," said Sugar Baby, the valedictorian.

"This aftah the rush hour, honkey," said Antwan.

"You not s'posed to be being hyeah," said Sugar Baby.

"I am sorry I do not speak English well," said the woman.

"Wha you got in that there bag?" said Sugar Baby.

"Old clothes which I mend," said the woman.

"You got bread?" asked Antwan. To her look of confusion, he explained: "Money?"

"I am a poor woman. I have just coins for my supper."

To this, Antwan took great umbrage and brought a flat smacking black hand across the woman's white face.

"Ah don't like liars. Ain't nobody tell you lying a sin?" asked Antwan.

"It shameful," said Sugar Baby and smacked her in the other direction.

"No. No. No. Do not hit," cried the woman as she tried to cover her head.

"Get yo' hand down," demanded Antwan, and he banged her a shot in the head. Then he tried his latest karate chop on her right shoulder, but a fist proved better. It knocked the babushka off and sent blood trickling from her right earlobe. Sugar Baby hoisted the old woman to her feet and rammed her head against the window behind the train seat while Antwan rummaged through her pockets. They got $1.17, so Sugar Baby hit her again for being so cheap.

They got off at the next stop, commenting on how they had made the subways once again free of whites after nightfall. It did not occur to them that they had also helped make the subway system of New York City equally free of blacks and Puerto Ricans after that hour. They watched the empty train roll by, headed for Mosholu Parkway, the last station on the D train with the next stop the open yards.

There was not much to do with $1.17, but they went upstairs to the street anyway. It was a white neighborhood, which meant the racist storeowners didn't have everything locked up or hidden away out of reach, as in the black neighborhoods. Antwan and Sugar Baby, free of this racist store-owner mentality, enjoyed themselves like free men in these stores and markets where goods were displayed openly for people to handle, inspect, and then decide upon purchasing. At the end of this small sojourn off the Grand Concourse, they had three cans of aerosol spray paint, three bottles of Coke, four Twinkies, eight candy bars, a nudie magazine, and a bar of Cashmere Bouquet soap. And they still had their $1.17 left.

"Wha you rip that soap off for?" demanded Sugar Baby.

"Maybe we can sell it," said Antwan.

"That stupid," said Sugar Baby. "Who gonna buy a bar of soap around our neighborhood?"

"We could use it, maybe?" said Antwan thoughtfully. He had seen a television show once where a woman ran water over soap and then rubbed the resulting foam onto her face.

"Wha fo?"

"With water and stuff," said Antwan.

"You dumb. That Uncle Tom stuff. You Uncle Tom," said Sugar Baby.

"Ah ain' no Tom," said Antwan. "Don' you call me no Tom."

"Then wah yo' doin' with soap?"

"Ah thought it was a candy bar, is all."

"Well, get rid of it."

Antwan threw it through the ground floor window of an apartment building and then they both ran, laughing. They had to run because, as everyone knew, racist cops would bust you for no reason at all.

There was a reason for the spray paint. Sugar Baby was one of the better artists at Martin Luther King. He had painted the ceiling of the gymnasium by hanging suspended by ropes one night with Antwan holding a flashlight from the floor below. And there it was for the big game against DeWitt Clinton. A masterpiece laid on a $30,000 acoustical ceiling. In red and green spray paint: SUGAR BABY.

"Beautiful," Antwan had said.

"Oh, no," the principal had said.

61

"Ah'm king lord over all de planet," Sugar Baby had said then, and now, running down a side street in the Bronx, he was going to do his masterwork. Instead of painting "Sugar Baby" on a ceiling or just one car of a subway train, he was going to invade the yards and put an entire train to his spray paint—if the cans lasted.

The yard stretched beside an elevated track, and in the darkness he could tell he would have his pick. He needed the right train, one which was without other's works, but it seemed impossible to find one free of "Chico," "RAM I," "WW," and "Joey 172."

Sugar Baby finally made the hard decision. He would paint over. To make the cans last, he decided to omit the usual border and substitute one long thin line in script. He was good at handwriting, making the best B's in the school, and a guidance counselor had told him his handwriting was good enough to make him the president of a college or at least of a corporation.

He was on the first loop of the S, a bright fluorescent green crescent, when a face popped out from between two cars. It was a white face. It was a man. Sugar Baby and Antwan started to run. Then they saw the man was alone. And he wasn't that big. Thin, in fact.

"Hi," said Remo.

"Who you, mother?" said Antwan.

"I'm looking for somebody," said Remo, and he hopped down off the car onto the cinders of the yard.

Neither Antwan nor Sugar Baby noticed that

this man landed on the crunchy cinders with the silence of a balloon touching felt.

"You looking for a bruisin'," said Sugar Baby.

"You grin, you in, mother," said Antwan.

"I really don't have time to rap," said Remo, "and I don't think coaxing will work."

Antwan and Sugar Baby giggled. They spread apart so Antwan could come at the front and Sugar Baby at the back. The white man stood quietly. Sugar Baby tried his karate chop. The hand came down perfect on the white man's head. He imagined himself splitting a brick. He imagined the head opening. He imagined how he would tell how he killed a honkey with one blow. His imaginings were interrupted by a decided pain in his right wrist. The skin was there but the fingers would not move, as if the hand were connected to the forearm by a bag of jelly. Sugar Baby dropped the spray paint. Antwan saw this and put his feet to action, heading out of the yards. He got four steps. On the fifth, his hip failed to cooperate. He went skin-splitting burning across the gravel, crying for his mother, professing innocence, vowing cooperation, and generally expressing fond feelings for the world and a desire to live in peace with all mankind.

"Who is Joey 172?" Remo asked.

"Ah don' know, man. Hey, ah square wif you, baby. Ah love you, baby," moaned Antwan.

"Try again," said Remo.

And Antwan felt a sharp stabbing pain in his neck but he saw no knife in the white man's hands.

"Don' know, man. Ah knows a Chico and a Ramad 85. They south city men."

"Joey 172, ever hear of him?"

"No, man. He nothing."

"Then you know him?"

"Ah say he nothing. Hey, Sugar Baby, tell mah man hyeah whuffo Joey 172."

"He nuffin'," said Sugar Baby, holding his painful right arm as vertical as possible. If he held it straight down and breathed very gently he could make the wrist pain almost bearable, if the elbow were cradled just right. When Sugar Baby said "nuffin'," he said it very softly.

"Where's he from?" Remo asked.

"Nowhere, man. He's nothing."

"Try," said Remo.

"Ah'm tryn, man. He ain' big enough to be from somewheres."

"Where's nowhere?" asked Remo.

"Lotsa places nowhere, man. You dumb or something?" said Sugar Baby.

"Name some," said Remo and gave Sugar Baby's dangling right arm a gentle touch.

Sugar Baby screamed. He suddenly remembered someone saying once that Joey 172 was from the Stuyvesant High School.

"All right, we'll all go there," said Remo.

"Bronx High School of Science," Sugar Baby corrected quickly. "He one of them Toms. Bronx High School of Science. Ah seen a Joey 172 there. They say that where he from."

"Are you sure?" asked Remo.

And even in the next great pain, Sugar Baby allowed as how nobody could be sure, and Antwan

64

too allowed as how it was probably Bronx High School of Science. Now, if the man wanted Chico, they could get him Chico for sure. Everybody knew Chico. For Chico they could give him the address.

"Thank you," said Remo.

As an afterthought he took the can of green glow spray paint and, ripping off their shirts, made a neat artistic "Remo" on each of their chests.

"I'm an artist myself," said Remo and went whistling off to find the Bronx High School of Science building, which as it turned out was nearby. On all the walls, there was no Joey 172. It was a big city and finding one graffiti artist in a plague of them was like singling out a locust in a swarm. And then he had an idea. He bought a can of white spray paint from a hardware store open late and convinced a cab driver to take him to Harlem. This required a fist full of twenty-dollar bills and a gentle stroking of the cab driver's neck. When Remo told the driver to let him off in front of an empty lot, the driver tried to nod but his neck hurt too much.

Remo skipped into the lot from the silent street. If night crime had thinned the street population of the rest of New York City, it had made Harlem into a desperately quiet enclave of citizens bunkered precariously for the night. Almost nothing moved except occasional packs of youngsters or convoys of grownups.

Stores were shuttered with metal shields, occasionally working streetlights illuminated empty littered sidewalks, a rat scurried soundlessly along a wall. And it was the wall Remo wanted.

Even in the dim half-light, he could make out the strong lines of powerful colors blending into a mosaic of fine black faces, set like a monument of a new generation against the decaying brick of a preceding one. It was a "wall of respect," and it hurt Remo a bit to deface it.

With the white paint, he sprayed a neat and glaring "Joey 172" across the wall and then faded back across the street to wait. The first person to spot the desecration of the wall that was, by custom and mutual consent, not to be touched was a youngster with a key around his neck. He stopped as if hit in the stomach with a pail of water. Remo lounged on a stoop. The gray dawn was succumbing to light. The youngster ran off. Remo smelled the ripe aroma of day-old greasy ribs, combined with week-old oranges and rotting chicken bones.

The street lights went off. The youngster came back with three others. By the time the sun was high, Remo had what he wanted. A large crowd formed in front of the wall spilling out into the street. Young men in gang jackets, older ones in rainbows of reds and yellows and platform shoes, a few winos careening precariously in place, a fat woman with layers of clothes like tenting over haystacks.

And down the street, his arms pinned by two burly men with raging Afroes, was a young man, his eyeglasses askew, his eyes wide with terror, his sneakers kicking helplessly in the air.

"That him," yelled a woman. "That Joey 172."

"Burn the mother," yelled a man.

"Cut him," shrieked a kid. "Cut him. Cut him good."

Remo eased himself from the stoop and cut into the mob, some of whom had been loudly discussing what to do about the white man across the street.

He wedged himself toward the opening where the two burly men were slapping the youngster into place. Remo cleared a small area in front of him quickly. To the crowd it looked like hands floating and bodies falling. The front of the crowd, after making some useless swings with knives and knuckles, tried to retreat from Remo. The back pushed forward and the front pushed back. Swinging started in the center of the crowd. Remo yelled for quiet. He wasn't heard.

"I don't suppose," he said, in a voice smothered to insignificance, like a pebble rolling uphill against an avalanche, "that you would consider this graffiti an expression of culture and ethnic pride?"

Not getting a response, he dropped the young man's handlers with two backhands flat to the side of the skull, just compressing the blood flow momentarily. Each dropped like a ripe plum. Remo grabbed the boy and cut his way through a wing of the crowd. Two blocks away, he avoided a police column that was waiting for the mob to fight out its energy before moving in.

"Hey, man, thanks," said the youngster.

"You're not going anywhere, kid," said Remo,

stopping the lad by cementing the boy's wrist to his palm. They were in a deserted alley now with crumbled bricks rising toward the end like refuse from a bombing raid.

"Are you the painter of the Joey 172's?" Remo asked.

"No, man, I swear it," said the boy. He was about twelve years old, a foot shorter than Remo. His Captain Kangaroo tee shirt was torn off his left side revealing a skinny chest and bony shoulders.

"All right," said Remo. "I'll take you back to the mob, then."

"I did it," said the boy.

"Now we're talking."

"But I didn't mess up no wall of respect, man."

"I know," said Remo. "I did it for you."

"You mother," said the boy. "What'd you do that for?"

"So that I could enlist the aid and resources of the community in meeting you."

"You ain't much with a spray can, man. You got a weak hand. A real weak hand."

"I never defaced anything before," said Remo.

"Why should I help you?" asked the boy logically.

"Because on one hand I'm going to give you two hundred dollars cash if you do, and on the other, I'm going to puncture your ear drums if you don't," said Remo, just as logically.

"You make a sweet offer. Where's the money?"

Remo took a wad of bills from his pocket and counted out exactly two hundred dollars.

"I'll be back in a minute," said the boy. "I just want to see if this money's real. Can't be too careful nowadays."

Remo took a flat hand and, pushing it up against the boy's spinal column like a concentrated jet of force, catapulted the boy into the air so the floppy sneakers paused momentarily above Remo's head.

"Eeeow," yelled the boy and felt himself turn over and head for the rubble below him, skull first, until he was caught like a parachute harness an eyelash away from ground collision and righted.

"Money's good," he said. "What can I do for you, friend?"

"I've got a problem," said Remo. "I'm looking for some people who are mad about something."

"I feel for those mothers, man," said the boy honestly.

"These people are mad over something you wrote 'Joey 172' on. Like the mob back there at the 'wall of respect.' "

"That's a mean group back there."

"This group is meaner," said Remo.

"Here's your money back, man," said the boy wisely.

"Wait. If I don't get them, sooner or later they're gonna get you."

"You're not gonna hand me over to them?"

"No," said Remo.

"Why not?" asked the boy. He cocked his head.

"Because they have pretty stiff penalties for defacing property."

69

"Like what?"

"Like they cut your heart out."

The boy whistled. "They the ones that offed the politician and the rich lady?"

Remo nodded.

The boy whistled again.

"I've got to know what you defaced."

"Improved," said the boy.

"All right, improved."

"Let's see. Bathrooms at school."

Remo shook his head.

"Two cars on an A train."

"I don't think so," said Remo.

"A bridge."

"Where?"

"Near Tremont Avenue. That's real uptown," said the boy.

"Any church or religious monument nearby?"

The boy shook his head.

"Did you do it on a painting or something?"

"I don't mess over someone else's work," said the boy. "Just things. Not works. Rocks and stuff."

"Any rocks?"

"Sure. I practice on rocks."

"Where?" asked Remo.

"Central Park once. Prospect Park a lot. Rocks are nothing, man."

"Any place else?"

"A museum. I did one on the big museum off Central Park. With the guy on the horse out front."

"What did the rock look like?" asked Remo.

"Big. Square like. With some circles and birds on it and stuff. A real old rock. The birds were shitty like some real little kid carved them."

"Thanks," said Remo.

Chapter Six

Off Central Park Remo found the Museum of
Natural History, a massive stone building with
wide steps and a bronze statue of Teddy Roosevelt
on a horse, facing fearlessly the onslaught of the
wilds, namely Fifth Avenue on the other side of
the park. The bronze Roosevelt presided over two
bronze Indians standing at his side, equally
fearless in their unchanging stare across the park.

Remo made a contribution at the entrance and
asked for the exhibit of stones. The clerk, drowsy
from the mind-smothering passing out of buttons,
which labeled the donor as one of those keenly
aware of the importance of nature and of the
Museum of Natural History, said the museum had
a lot of stones. Which one did he want?

"A big one," said Remo. "One that has some graffiti on it."

"We don't feature graffiti, sir," said the clerk.

"Well, do you have any stones? Large ones?" asked Remo. He felt heat rising in his body, not because the afternoon was muggy but because if the organization was still operating, they could probably have had this whole thing worked out in an afternoon and just given him the name of whoever or whatever he was supposed to connect with, and that would be that. Now he was looking for rocks in a museum. If he were right, he would have this whole little mess wrapped up in a day. Give him the sacred rock and the killers would have to come to him.

"We don't just collect rocks, sir," said the clerk.

"This is a special rock. It's got engraving on it."

"Oh. You mean the South American artifacts. That's the ground floor. Turn right."

Remo wandered past a stuffed bear, an imitation jungle, two dried musk oxen, and a stuffed yak eating a plastic peony into a dark room with large stones. All were intricately carved. Massive heads with flattened noses and almond eyes. Curving serpents weaving among stilted birds. Rock remnants of peoples who had disappeared in the western onslaught. But as Chiun had said, "The sword does not destroy a people; only a better life does. Swords kill. They do not change."

But on South American cultures Chiun had never shed any light, and Remo was sure it was because those cultures had been cut off from the rest of the world until the coming of the Euro-

73

peans in 1500. Which meant to Chiun, since an ancestor had probably never done business there, that the area was still undiscovered.

"You mean you didn't have book on any of them," Remo had said.

"I mean the area is undiscovered," said Chiun. "A wilderness with strange people, like your country, until I came. Although your birthplace is easier because of so many descendants of Europeans and Africans. But now that I have discovered it, future generations of Sinanju will know of your inscrutable nation."

"And what about South America?" Remo had asked.

"So far undiscovered," Chiun had said. "If you should find out anything, let me know."

Now Remo was in the museum, finding out, and finding out very little at that. The carvings seemed very Egyptian, yet Egyptians used softer stone. These stones were hard.

Two guards stood before a large unmarked door at the north end of the display room.

"I'm looking for a special stone," Remo said. "It's been marked over recently."

"You can't go in," said one guard.

"So it's in there?"

"I ain't saying that. Anyone who goes in needs special permission from the Antiquities Department."

"And where's the Antiquities Department?"

"That's closed today. Just the assistant is on."

"Where's the department?"

"Don't bother, mister. They won't let you in.

74

They never let anybody in who just walks up anymore. Just special people. Don't bother."

"I want to bother," Remo said.

The assistant was in a small box of an office with a desk that made moving around difficult. She looked up from a document, focusing above blue-framed eyeglasses. Her reddish hair formed a bouquet around her delicate face.

"He's not in and I'm busy," she said.

"I want to see that stone in the locked room."

"That's what I said. He's not in and I'm busy."

"I don't know who you're talking about," Remo said, "but I just want to see that stone."

"Everybody who sees it goes through the director, James Willingham. And he's not in as I said."

"I'm not going through James Willingham, I'm going through you."

"He'll be back tomorrow."

"I want to see it today."

"It's really nothing much. It hasn't even been classified into a culture yet."

Remo leaned across the desk and, holding her eyes with his, smiled ever so slightly. She blushed.

"C'mon," he whispered in a voice that stroked her.

"All right," she said, "but only because you're sexy. Academically this makes no sense."

Her name was Valerie Garner. She had an M.A. from Ohio State and was working toward her Ph.D at Columbia. She had everything in her life but a real man. She explained this on the way down to the South American exhibit area. There were no real men left in New York City, she said.

"All I want," she said plaintively, "is someone who is strong but gentle, sensitive to my needs, who will be there when I want and not be there when I don't want. Do you see? Is that asking too much?" asked Valerie.

"Yes," said Remo, beginning to suspect that Valerie Garner, assuming she ever met a man, would not be able to see him because the sound waves rising incessantly from her mouth would obscure her vision.

Valerie motioned the guards away from the door and unlocked it with a key from around her neck.

"The director goes bananas about this stone and there's no reason for it. It's nothing. Nothing."

The nothing she described was about Remo's height. It rested on a polished pink marble pedestal with soft crystal lights bathing it in a deep artificial glow like a far-off morning. A small flowing fountain, carved from what appeared to be a solid five-foot piece of jade, bubbled gently, its clear water coming from carved lips above a perfectly round basin.

The stone itself looked like a random block of igneous rock with incredibly inept scratching of circles and lines, and only by the greatest tolerance could Remo make out a circle, birds, snakes, and what might have been a human head with feathers above it. But the rock had what Remo wanted.

A graceful, glowing green signature of "Joey 172" ran diagonally across the circle from the chunky snake to the stiff bird.

"The graffiti is the only piece of art in it," said Valerie.

"I think so, too," said Remo, who had seen enough. The stone looked like the symbol in the note the police had recovered from under Mrs. Delpheen's body, the symbol that was called an Uctut in the other eleven languages of the note.

"You should have seen Willingham when he saw the graffiti on it," Valerie was babbling. "He couldn't talk for an hour. Then he went into his office and stayed on the phone for a half-day. A full half-day. Long distance calls, overseas and everything. More than a thousand dollars in phone calls that one afternoon."

"How do you know?" asked Remo.

"I handle the budget. I thought we were going to get killed by the trustees but they approved it. Even approved two guards for the doors. And look at the stone. It's nothing."

"Why do you say that?" Remo asked.

"For one thing, I don't think it's more than a thousand years old, which would therefore not justify such shoddy craftsmanship. For a second, look at the Aztec and Inca work outside. Now those are gorgeous. This looks like a scribble compared to them. But you want to know something crazy?"

"Of course," said Remo, sidestepping Valerie's hand, which somehow alighted on his fly as she said the word "crazy."

"This stone has had more groups of visitors from all over the world than any other special exhibit. There's no reason for it."

77

"I think there is," Remo said. "Why didn't you people clean off the graffiti?"

"I tried to suggest that but Willingham wouldn't hear of it."

"Can you reach him today?"

"He never comes in on his day off. He's got an estate up in Westchester. You can't pry him out with crowbars."

"Tell him someone is defacing the statue."

"I can't do that. I'd be fired."

With two fingers, half curled and pressed together like a single instrument, Remo snapped his nails downward across the raised circle, carved by stone implements in a time that preceded even the memory of the Actatl tribe. Crumpled chunks of pinkish rock sprayed from the path of his fingers. A small white scar the size of an electric cord cut a curve in the circle.

"Now you've done it," said Valerie, pressing her hand to her forehead. "Now you've done it. This place is going to be a madhouse."

"You're going to phone Willingham, right?" said Remo pleasantly.

"Right. Get out of here. You don't know what you've done."

"I think I do," Remo said.

"Look," Valerie said, pointing to the scar. "That's bad enough. But if you're still here, there may be murder."

Remo shrugged. "Phone," he said.

"Get out of here."

"No," said Remo.

"You're too cute to die."

"I'm not leaving."

78

Since he was thin and Valerie was one of the toughest defensive guards in field hockey at Wellesley, she put her shoulder into his back and pushed. The back didn't move. She knew he couldn't weigh more than 150 pounds, so she tried again, this time getting a running start and throwing her body at the back.

When she was bracing for the thump of impact, it seemed as if the back suddenly dropped beneath her and she was hurtling horizontally toward a wall, and just as suddenly there were hands about her waist, soft hands that seemed to caress her as they guided her softly to her feet again.

"Make love, not war," said Valerie.

"Phone Willingham."

"Do that thing with the hands again."

"Later," Remo said.

"Just a touch."

"Later, I'll give you everything you want."

"There's no man who has that much."

Remo winked. Valerie glanced down at his fly.

"You're not one of those machismo types who's great with his fists and duds out in bed, are you?"

"Get Willingham and then find out."

"There won't be anything left of you. I mean it," said Valerie and with a shrug she went to the wall with a green metal cabinet. The cabinet housed a phone.

"It's not bad enough this rock's had to have running water in the room, but it's got its own private line, too. You ought to see the phone bills that come off of this line. It's incredible. Visitors come and make these free calls at museum expense and Willingham doesn't do anything about it."

Valerie's conversation with Willingham quickly dissolved into her pleas for Mr. Willingham to stop screaming. Waiting for him to arrive, Valerie took eighteen drinks of water, fourteen cigarettes, often lighting three at a time, went to the lavatory twice, and muttered "Oh God, what have we done?" every seven minutes.

Willingham was there in an hour.

He spotted the stone immediately. He was a large lumbering man with large freckles suntickled from their winter hibernation. He wore a tan suit and a blue ascot.

"Oh," he said, and "no" he said. His dark brown eyes rolled back into his forehead, and he weaved momentarily in place. He shook his head and gasped.

"No," he said firmly, and as his body regained its normal circulation, his lips tightened. His eyes narrowed and he moved methodically to the stone, ignoring Valerie and Remo.

He lowered himself to both knees and pressed his head to the marble base three times. Then with great force of will he turned to Valerie and asked: "When did you discover this?"

"When I did it," Remo said cheerily.

"You did this? Why did you do this?" Willingham asked.

"I didn't think it was a true yearning of man's cosmic consciousness," said Remo.

"How could you do it?" asked Willingham. "How? How?"

So Remo pressed two fingers tight together in a

light curve and with the same loose wristed snap made another line through the circle on the great stone. It crossed the first line at right angles, leaving an X.

"That's how," Remo said. "It's really not too hard. The secret, as in all better use of your body, is in breathing and rhythm. Breathing and rhythm. It looks fast, but it's really a function of the slowness of your hand being slower than the rock. You might say the rock moves out of the way of your fingers."

And with snapping fingers and rock dust flying from the great stone, Remo carved neatly through the spray of Joey 172 and the stiff bird and the curving raised snake: REMO.

"I can do it left-handed, too," he said.

"Ohhh," moaned Valerie, covering her eyes.

Willingham only nodded silently. He backed out of the display room and shut the door behind him. Remo heard a whirring. A large steel sheet descended from the ceiling, coming to a neat clicking stop at the floor. The room was sealed.

"Damn," said Valerie, running to the phone in the wall. She dialed. "I'm getting the police," she said to Remo over her shoulder. "This place is built like a walk-in safe. We'll never get out. Can't reason with Willingham after your insanity. He'll leave us here to rot. Why did you do it?"

"I wanted to express myself," said Remo.

"The line's dead," said Valerie. "We're trapped."

"Everyone is trapped," said Remo, remembering a talk long ago in which Chiun had explained confinement. "The only difference between people is in the size of their trap."

"I don't need philosophy. I need to get out of here."

"You will," said Remo. "But your fear isn't working for you."

"Another religious nut, like Willingham and his rock. Why do I always meet them?" asked Valerie. She sat down on the pedestal of the great stone. Remo sat down next to her.

"Look. All your life you've been trapped. Everyone is."

She shook her head. "Not buying," she said.

"If you're poor, you can't afford to travel, so you're trapped in your home town. If you're rich, you're trapped on earth unless you're an astronaut. And even they are trapped by the air they have to bring with them. They can't leave their suits or their ship. But even more than that, every human being is trapped by his life. We're surrounded on one end by our birth and the other by our death. We can't get out of our lives. These walls are just a small period in our trapped lives anyhow, see?"

"I need a way out of here, and you're giving me a pep talk."

"I could get you out of anything but your ignorance," Remo said, and it surprised him how much like Chiun he was sounding.

"Get me out of here."

"I will after I'm finished with it," said Remo.

"What do you mean by that?"

"I'm the one who's got Willingham and his friends trapped."

"Oh, Jesus," said Valerie. "Now not only are we trapped, Willingham is too."

"Exactly," said Remo. "He's trapped by his devotion to this ugly hunk of stone back here. I've got him."

"I'd rather be him," said Valerie, and she lowered her head into her hands and moaned about how she always met them. From the man in Paterson, New Jersey, who had to strap on a five foot medieval sword before he could get it up, to the Brooklyn dishwasher who had to lather her up with foaming Liquicare before he would do it. And now, the worst. Locked in a disguised safe with a guy who thinks the outside world is trapped because they have a rock inside with them.

"Why do I always meet them?" screamed Valerie, and she knew her screams would not be heard because the whole freaking room was lined with lead. They had even sealed off the beautiful north windows. Willingham had muttered something about protection from the north wind as though the ugly box of a rock was going to catch a headcold.

"Why me, Lord?" cried Valerie Gardner. "Why me?"

"Why not you?" asked Remo just as logically, and when he tried to comfort her with his hands, she shrugged away, saying she would rather do it with a walrus in aspic than with Remo.

Her anger turned to boredom and she started yawning. She asked Remo what time it was.

"Late," he said. "We've been here about five

83

hours and forty-three minutes. It's eight-thirty-two and fourteen seconds."

"I didn't see you look at a watch," Valerie said.

"I'm the best watch there is," said Remo.

"Oh, great," said Valerie, and she curled up in front of the stone and dozed off. An hour later, the square metal slab locking them in raised with a whirring sound. Valerie woke up. Remo smiled.

"Mr. Willingham, thank god," said Valerie, and then she shook her head. Mr. Willingham was nude except for a loincloth and a draping of yellow feathers in a robe around his body. He carried a stone knife in front of him. Six men followed him. Two ran to Valerie, throwing her to the floor and pinning her arms. The other four rushed to Remo, two grabbing one foot each and the other two going for his wrists.

"Hi, fellas," Remo said. He let himself be lifted. They brought him to the very top of the stone called Uctut. Willingham approached, the knife held high. He spoke in a language Remo couldn't recognize. It sounded like stone clicking against stone, popping sounds with the tongue of a language kept in secret over the centuries.

"Your heart will not recompense your foul deed for it is not enough for the desecration you have performed," said Willingham in English.

"I thought I improved the stone," Remo said.

"No, Mr. Willingham, no," cried Valerie. The two men stuffed part of their robes in her mouth.

"You may save yourself pain if you tell us the truth," said Willingham.

"I like pain," Remo said.

The man on his right wrist was gripping too

tightly and would lose control of his strength shortly. The one on the left was too loose, and the men at Remo's feet had no protection from his yanking his legs back and driving their ribcages into their intestines if he wished. He did not wish—yet.

"If you do not give me the information I seek, we will kill the girl," said Willingham.

"That's even better than giving me pain. I can live with that," said Remo.

"We will kill her horribly," said Willingham.

"What will be will be," said Remo philosophically.

He glanced down over the stone edge to the floor, where Valerie tried desperately to shake loose. Her face turned purple in fear and rage and hysteria.

"Let her go," said Remo, "and I'll tell you everything you want to know."

"Why you did this awful thing and everything?" asked Willingham.

"And even where you can reach Joey 172," said Remo.

"We know where we can reach Joey 172. We've known since the day after he did his horror. It is for the American people to make restitution, not us. Uctut wants proper restitution, not for his priests to soil their hands with unclean blood, but for the people of the offender to offer up to us the offender. To make the sacrifice through our hands but not by our hands."

"Why didn't you say so?" said Remo, feigning an air of enlightenment. "Through your hands but not by your hands. Now everything is crystal as cement. Through, not by. Why are we even arguing? Why didn't I see this before? And here I was thinking it was simple revenge."

"We have restored the sacrifices and will continue to do so until America acts properly," said Willingham.

"Would you like the Attorney General to hold down Joey 172 while the Secretary of State rips out his heart? Like you did to the congressman and Mrs. Delpheen?"

"They were in charge of monuments here at the museum. They refused my request to station guards in this room. And thus the desecration followed. It was their failure."

"Just who the hell do you expect to take this revenge for the writing on the stone?" Remo asked. "The FBI, the CIA? The Jersey City Police Department?"

"You have secret agencies. It could be done. We know it could be done. But your government has to realize what it has allowed to happen and then set about making amends. We would have allowed your government to do this quietly. Your government has done this before, many times and secretly. But your government has not acted to avenge the insult upon Uctut."

Remo noticed that Willingham held the stone knife in a strange grip. The back of the thumbnail drove the handle tight against the inside pads of the other fingers. From Orient to Western Europe, there was no grip like it. Not the Mecs in Paris or the stiletto in Naples. Even the many variations of tuck fist grip so prevalent in the American west, never used the thumb as the compressor. And yet this was a highly logical grip for a blade, allowing a good downward stroke.

Remo saw it coming from Willingham's flabby stomach, the slight twitch that meant he was getting his back into the thrust. And then he stopped at the top of the stroke as if generating power, which would be logical because a stone knife needed tremendous force to crack a chestbone.

"Now," said Willingham, his body tightened like a spring on the flicker of explosion. "Who sent you?"

"Snow White and the seven dwarfs. Or is it dwarves?"

"We will mutilate Valerie."

"You'd do that to your assistant?"

"I would do anything for my Uctut."

"Why do you call it Uctut? What does Uctut mean?" asked Remo.

"It is not the real name of the stone, but it is the name that men are privileged to speak," said Willingham. "We will mutilate Valerie."

"Only if you promise to start with her mouth," said Remo.

The stone knife hitched and started down with Willingham's shoulder under it. The thrust was perfect, except the body didn't cooperate. For the first time since the great stone had been served by the people of the Actatl, an Actatl knife struck the stone itself.

Remo's two feet yanked back, drawing the robed priests with them, and when his heels drove into their chests, they were going forward into the blows. Blood exploded out of their mouths with bits of lung. The two men holding his arms

87

felt themselves yanked over his body, and Remo was on his feet, softly on the pedestal as the Actatl knife committed the sacrilege of striking Uctut, the stone which it served.

Using thumbs brought together from a wide inward arc, Remo caught the soft temples of the two men pinning Valerie. The thumbs went in up to the index fingers, touched hair, and then squished out. The men were dead in the midst of holding, and they looked up dumbly, their eyes focused on eternity, their minds shattered midthought.

The men who had held Remo's arms were still dazed, crawling on the floor, looking for their balance. Remo snapped one vertebra on one man, and he suddenly stopped crawling and flattened out on the floor. His legs stopped responding, and shortly thereafter his brain stopped, too.

Remo dropped the other man with a short shattering chop to the forehead. The blow itself did not kill. It was designed to use the thick part of the skull as fragments, driving them into the frontal lobes. It did the job without getting the hands sticky.

Remo wiped his thumbs off on the golden feathers of the robe. He noticed the knots tying the feathers into the cape were strange. He had never seen knots like that before. He knew something about knots, too.

Valerie spit feathers out of her mouth. She coughed. She brushed herself off. She spit again.

"Fucking lunatics," she muttered.

Remo went over to Willingham who leaned against the stone like a man having a heart attack. His cheek pressed against the uppermost bird, his robe drawn tightly over his chest.

"Hi," said Remo. "Now we can talk."

"With my own hand I have desecrated Uctut," moaned Willingham.

"Now let's start at the beginning," said Remo. "This stone is Uctut, right?"

"This stone is the life of my fathers and their fathers before them. This stone is my people. In many skins and many colors are my people because you would not let us keep our own skins and our own hair and our own eyes. But our souls have never changed, and they reside in the infinite strength of our beautiful god, who is eternal and one with his people, who serve him."

"You're talking about the rock?" asked Remo.

"I talk about that which is us."

"All right," said Remo. "We got the rock is holy. And you people are the Actatl and you worship it, right?"

"Worship? You make it sound like lighting some candle or not playing with women. You do not know worship until your very life is sacrifice."

"Right, right," said Remo. "Moving right along, we know you killed the congressman and Mrs. Delpheen. What I don't know is why I never heard of you guys before."

"Our protection was your lack of knowledge of us."

"You keep talking about other skins. What does that mean?"

"You would not let us keep our own skins. If I were brown with high cheekbones as once the Actatl were, would I be a director of this museum? Would DeSen or DePanola be ranking generals in the armies of France and Spain?"

"They're Actatl, too?" said Remo.

"Yes," said Willingham. He looked past Remo at the bodies on the floor, and his voice trailed off like an echo. "They came with me."

"I don't think they're ranking now," said Remo, glancing at the stone dead stillness of the bodies, limp as leftover string beans.

"Would we have been able to worship our precious and awesome stone in your society? People are not allowed to worship stones."

"I take it you've never been to the Vatican or the Wailing Wall or Mecca," said Remo.

"Those are symbols. They do not worship them. This stone god we worship and would never have been allowed to love and serve it as we do."

"Are there a lot of you Actatl?"

"Enough," said Willingham. "Always enough. But we made a mistake."

"Yeah?"

"We did not find out who you were."

"I'm your friendly neighborhood assassin," said Remo.

"They will find you and destroy you. They will tear your limbs. They will obliterate you. For we Actatl have survived the test and we are strong and we are many and we are disguised."

"You're also as flimsy as dandelions," said Remo. He noticed the separations in Willingham's lower teeth oozed red, threatening to spill over his lower lip.

"We will survive. We have survived five

90

hundred years," said Willingham, and he smiled, releasing the dam of blood over his lips, and let his yellow feathered robe slide from his shoulders. The handle of the stone knife, a round block of chipped stone, stuck from his belly and underneath his heart. Willingham, who was so expertly trained to rip out the hearts of others, had missed his own and was bleeding to death.

"I have bad news for you," said Remo. "I come from a house thousands of years old. While your Actatl had yet to use the stone, Sinanju was. Before Rome, Sinanju was. Before the Jews wandered in the desert, Sinanju was."

"You have taken other skins, too, to survive?" Willingham hissed.

"No," said Remo.

"Eeeeah," cried Willingham. "We are doomed."

"Hopefully," said Remo. "Now where is your headquarters?"

And then Willingham smiled his death smile. "We are not doomed. Thank you for telling me so."

Willingham went down in a mess of blood and feathers as though he were a goose caught at close range by double barrels of birdshot. Valerie spat the last feather out of her mouth.

"You were going to let them mutilate me, weren't you?"

"Only your mouth," said Remo.

"Men are turds," yelled Valerie.

"Shhh," said Remo. "We've got to get out of here."

"You're damned right. I'm calling the police."

"I'm afraid you're not," said Remo and touched

91

a spot on the left side of her throat. She tried to speak, but all that came out was a dry gurgle.

Remo led her from the room. Under a painting on the wall outside he found the switch that lowered the steel door. He heard it thump and click into place, then he closed the wooden outside doors. On the door he hung a sign he took from a nearby men's room: CLOSED FOR REPAIRS.

Then Remo led Valerie from the darkened, closed-for-the-night museum and delivered her to the hotel where Chiun and he were staying at Fifty-ninth Street and Columbus Circle. Then he massaged her throat in such a way that her voice came back.

Chiun sat in the middle of the living room of the suite. Bobbi Delpheen practiced her new forehand stroke, allowing the racket to float into an imaginary ball.

"You here for tennis lessons, too?" Bobbi asked Valerie.

"The world is mad," shrieked Valerie.

"Shut up or your voice goes again," said Remo.

"They've got a great system," Bobbi reassured the worried Valerie. "You don't hit the ball. The racket hits it."

Quietly, Valerie began to cry. She would have preferred screaming, but she did not like being voiceless.

Remo spoke softly to Chiun. He told him of the stone. He told him of the new grip on the knife. He told him of Willingham's sudden last joy when he had asked for the location of the Actatl headquarters.

Chiun thought a moment.

' "That lunatic Smith has led us into ruin," he said.

"You saying we should run?"

"The time to run has passed. The time to attack has begun. Except we cannot attack. He smiled when you asked about his headquarters because I am sure he does not have one. We are set against the worst of all enemies, the formless unknown."

"But if they are unknown to us, we are unknown to them, Little Father," said Remo.

"Perhaps," said Chiun. "Once, many of what you call your centuries ago, there was a Master, and he did disappear for many years, and the stories were told that he had gone to a new world, but he was not believed because he was much given to exaggeration."

"So?"

"I must search my memory," said Chiun, "and see if something there may help us." And he was quiet. Very quiet.

"Can I talk now?" said Valerie.

"No," said Remo. Valerie started crying again.

Remo looked out over the night lights of Central Park. His plan had worked so well until Willingham. When you grabbed hold of an organization, you planned on working your way to the top. You didn't expect someone to kill himself along the way and break the chain.

Remo walked away from the window. Chiun had often warned him against thinking too much, lest his greater senses be dulled to the subtleties of the moment.

And in this way Remo did not see the binoculars trained on the window of his hotel suite. He did not see the man raise a rifle, then lower it.

"I can't miss," said the man to another person in the room across the street from Remo's.

"Wait until you're inside the room. We want his heart," said the other man.

"Willingham probably couldn't miss either. But this guy came out of the museum and Willingham didn't," the second man said.

"I still can't miss."

"Wait until you're inside his room. We want his heart," said the second man. "When we get the word."

Chapter Seven

The spectacular failure at the Museum of Natural History was outlined in detail to a senior vice-president of a computer company branch office, Paris, Rue St. Germain.

Monsieur Jean Louis Raispal deJuin, vice-president for corporate development of international data and research, nodded with all the feigned interest his finely etched patrician face could muster. Uncle Carl, from the German side of the family, had always been rather peculiar and one had to be patient with him. Jean Louis reacted instinctively with the politeness beaten into him by his governess and ordered by his mother, who had always said one could not choose one's family, but one could certainly choose one's manners.

So Jean Louis listened on about all sorts of mayhem and two formidable Americans, except one was an Oriental, and all the while his mind worked at an adjustment he would make in a research team that was stymied by a computer problem.

Occasionally he glanced out at Rue St. Germain with its bookshops and restaurants. He had always considered his university days his happiest, and since his work was entirely cerebral and could be done anywhere, the firm had allowed him to select the office site and furnishings, which were largely Napoleonic period combined with Chinese. The ornate gilded forms mixed so well. Robust, mother had called them.

Uncle Carl sat on a chair, ignoring the center extended portion of the seat, which allowed men to sit sideways so that their sword pommels could hang conveniently across their laps. Uncle Carl sweated like a stuffed red sausage this fine autumnal day, and Jean Louis wished he would suggest a walk, perhaps in the direction of Invalides, where Napoleon was buried, along with all those who had directed la belle France in one disastrous war after another. Uncle Carl liked those things. Even though he often railed about things European and often trailed off into some South American nonsense. This was surprising because Uncle Carl was an ardent Nazi, and it had taken awesome family pull to get him off unindicted by the War Crimes panels. Fortunately Cousin Geoffrey was a lieutenant general on Field Marshal

Montgomery's staff and Uncle Bill was in the American OSS.

Jean Louis deJuin had been a teenager at the time, during the German occupation of Paris, and even though Cousin Michel was on the most wanted list as a leader in the Maquis resistance movement, Jean Louis' family had lived quite well during the occupation, by some order from within the German general staff.

As mother had said, one did not choose one's family, and Jean Louis had thought little about it until now, when Uncle Carl said those strange words.

"So now it is up to you, Jean Louis Raispal de-Juin."

"What is up to me, dear Uncle?" asked Jean Louis.

"Our hopes, our fortunes, our honor, and our very survival."

"Ah well, very good," said Jean Louis. "Would you care for coffee?"

"Have you been listening?"

"Yes, but of course," said Jean Louis. "Terrible happenings. Life can be so cruel."

"Willingham is gone now."

"The pale fellow who worked in the museum?"

"He was the foremost priest," said Uncle Carl.

"Of what?" asked Jean Louis.

Uncle Carl's face burst crimson. He slammed a large fat fist down on the pressed leather of an eighteenth century desk. Jean Louis blinked. Uncle Carl was getting violent.

"Don't you know who you are? What your family is? Where you came from? Your roots?"

97

"We share some great, great, great uncle who was in South America for a while. Is that what you mean? Please don't be violent. Perhaps some anisette, Uncle?"

"Jean Louis, tell me now, for this answer must be truthful . . ."

"Yes, Uncle Carl."

"When we took those walks when you were a child, and I told you things about your ancestors, was your mind paying attention to me, Jean Louis? Tell me truthfully now."

"Well, you know how children are, Uncle Carl."

"The truth."

"No, Uncle Carl. I went with you because as a German you could get the best patisserie at the time. I thought about chocolate."

"And the manuscripts I gave you?"

"I must confess, I drew pictures on them. Paper was scarce, Uncle Carl."

"And the name of our possession? That all of us share?"

"That stone. Uctut?"

"Yes. Its real name," said Uncle Carl.

"I forgot, Uncle Carl."

"I see," said Carl Johann Liebengut, president of Bavarian Electronics Works. "So you think I am a German uncle of a French nephew, and this is such a fine autumn day, what is this crazy uncle doing talking about death in New York City, yes?"

"You put it rather harshly, Uncle."

"True, no?"

"All right, true," said Jean Louis. His gray vest tailored precisely to his lean form hardly wrinkled as he brought one leg over the other and formed an arch with his long delicate fingers in front of his face. He rested his chin on this arch.

"You are no more French than I am German, Jean Louis," said Carl Johann Liebengut, and such was the coolness of his voice that deJuin forgot about the sunshine and the bookstores and the autumn green of the leaves outside on Rue St. Germain.

"I said you are not French," said Carl.

"I heard you," said deJuin.

"You are Actatl."

"You mean, I share a bit of this blood."

"Actatl is what you are. Everything else is a disguise because the world would not let you be Actatl."

"My father is a deJuin. So am I."

"Your father was a deJuin and he gave you that disguise. Your mother gave you the blood. I gave you the knowledge, and you apparently rejected it. I am too old to wage the war of survival that is now required, and you, Jean Louis, apparently do not want to. So a thousand years of our heritage, maybe more, dies this day. Monsieur deJuin, may you have a long and happy life. I go."

"Uncle Carl, wait."

"For what, Monsieur deJuin?"

"For me to listen. Come, I will go with you. If I was unattentive as a child, let me listen now. I am not saying I will take up the standards of the war of our tribe, but I am saying I will not let a millenia of history succumb without even access to my ear."

99

As a child, the tale of the last king of the Actatl has amused Jean Louis because of the discrepancies of his childhood memory—the attenuation of unimportant things.

They walked along Rue St. Germain, up the Left Bank, past restaurants and cinemas and coffee shops and tobacco shops, strung along the way like so many minor potholes to collect loose change. At Rue du Bac, they turned right and crossed the Seine over the Pont Royal Bridge. Now as deJuin heard the story of the last king he could appreciate the man's brilliant assessment of a sociological avalanche, one that would crush the existing Indian culture to pumice. The Maya had not known this. The Inca had not known this, nor had the all-powerful Aztec. And they were no more.

But here was Uncle Carl, talking to him about symbols on a sacred stone. Every nuance, every meaning was as clear as on the day the priests of the Actatl had made their last sacrifice in the verdant Mexican hills.

"Why have we not made sacrifices until recently?" asked deJuin. "Back in our ancestors' time, it was a monthly thing. And now we use it only for revenge?"

"It was not thought wise on one hand. And on the other, the sacrifice of the last of the Actatl city was interpreted as the final eternal sacrifice. But if you should look upon the stone and see the living lines as I have done, if you had gone last year as you were supposed to, you would have seen everything in the stone. The meaning of the earth and rivers and sky. To see everything we have heard about. There it is, our history. Shared by no one else, Jean Louis. Ours. You don't know how insufferable those Nazi rallies were, but I had to do it for the tribe, just in case Hitler should win. What had started out as a protection society for the tribe eventually became a network of each of us helping the other. Then came the desecration of Uctut."

"And just the death of this one boy would not do?"

"Of course not. First, Uctut demands that the United States bear the responsibility for the desecration. And what is the life of a Negro worth?"

"You forget, our real skin is brown, Uncle," said deJuin.

"Have you decided to take up the case of our family?"

"I want to show you something," Jean Louis said. "That is all. Do you know why I went into computers?"

"No," said the older man, who was having difficulty keeping up with the long strides of the tall, thin man who moved so effortlessly and so quickly while seeming just to stroll.

"Because, it was untainted by what has made me feel uncomfortable all my life. Computers were pure. I will now show you what is not pure for me."

And this bridge led to the Louvre, a giant square of a castle with an immense courtyard that had been transformed into a museum more than two hundred years before. A gaggle of Japanese tourists coming on in phalanx marched into a side exhibit following a leader with a flag.

Four Americans laughing noisily brushed aside a vendor who offered to take their pictures.

"It takes a full week just to properly peruse, not even to examine, the contents of this museum," said deJuin.

"We don't have a week," said Uncle Carl.

The younger man smiled. "We don't need a week." He spread his right arm slowly in a wide arc, as if offering the entire museum. "I spent, if you would total the time, literally months here in my student days. China, ancient Greece, Europe, even some modern South American painters are all represented here."

"Yes, yes." Carl was becoming impatient.

"I never felt at home with any of them. None. Since childhood, even though Father told me our family went back to Charlemagne, I never felt at home in France. I felt a little bit at home in computers because it was a life without a past."

"So what are you saying?"

"I am saying, dear Uncle, that I am no European."

"So you will help?"

"Help, yes. Run at someone with a stone knife, no."

Uncle Carl became flustered. He angrily announced he had not come to Paris to organize a committee but to seek help in fighting a holy war of the tribe.

"And how is that war going, Uncle?"

"Disastrous," said Carl.

"So let us get it going right, eh? Come. We think."

"The knife is holy," said Carl, lest his nephew think he was surrendering a point.

"Success is holier," said Jean Louis deJuin. He looked around the spacious and awesomely elegant stone courtyard of the Louvre for the last time as a Frenchman and silently said his goodbye to Europe in his heart.

Listening to Uncle Carl, it did not take deJuin long to see what had gone wrong with the family. The Actatl had been content to hide, not only for generations, but for centuries, and when a time came that action was demanded, action was beyond the capacity of the family.

He hailed a cab and ordered it to the small apartment he kept for his mistress on Avenue de-Bretuil, a spacious two floors of rooms with large rococco molding on the ceiling. The houseboy, a North African dressed in a silver embroidered waistcoat, served them coffee with heavy dollops of sweet cream. Uncle Carl ate three patisserie, gleaming in syrupy sugar over candied fruit set in an exquisitely light flaky crust, while Jean Louis took a pad from his pocket and wrote down several formulas. DeJuin, oblivious to his uncle, did not answer questions about what he was doing. At one point, he phoned into his office and asked for computer time. He read several formulas to an assistant over the phone and fifteen minutes later got his answer.

"Ordure," he mumbled when he got the answer. He tore up his notes, flinging them into the air. The houseboy attempted to pick up the pieces, and deJuin shooed him from the room. He paced. And as he paced he talked.

103

"The trouble, dear Uncle Carl, is that the tribe is not fit to rule." He went on without waiting for an answer.

"We have hidden so long that when the moment comes when we must make a just demand, not only is it ignored, but we do not even know how to make it. All has been disaster, from start to finish."

Jean Louis deJuin walked to the window and looked out onto the sunlit street.

"What must we do?" asked Uncle Carl.

"We start over," said deJuin. "From now on, the goal of the Actatl is power. In the future, when our names are known, our demands will be met."

"What of our demands for reparation?" asked Carl.

"From the beginning that was stupid," said de-Juin. "The notes demanding reparations were unclear. Written in twelve languages and none of them English. Forget that. We ourselves will take care of the reparations at the proper time. But our main problem now is these two very dangerous men, the American and the Oriental."

DeJuin drummed on the crystal bright window pane with his fingers as he talked.

"We were unlucky that we bumped into them," said Carl.

"No," said deJuin. "They came looking for us, and like fools, we went rushing into their trap. There is one highly probable course of events, and this is it: After the descration of Uctut, our actions in the sacrifices somehow stepped on something or someone in a highly sensitive area that employs killers. Men of that skill do not just go wandering into museums on pleasure trips. We must have caused a danger to them. Now, whoever or whatever we have endangered wants us to attack those two. They could hope for nothing better. We will attack, and we will be destroyed."

"So we will not attack?" said Uncle Carl.

"No. We *will* attack. But we will attack our way, on our terms, at our time. And we will use these killers as they would use us. We will trace from them the secret organization they work for, and then we will seize that organization's power. That power will become the tribe's power, and then the Actatl will hide no more."

DeJuin paused at the window, waiting for a comment from Uncle Carl. But there was only silence.

When he turned, he saw that Carl had gotten off his chair and was kneeling on the floor, his head touching the carpet, his arms extended in front of him.

"What is this, Uncle Carl?"

"You are king," Carl said. "You are king." Carl looked up. "Come to me."

DeJuin moved close to the older man, and Carl leaned forward and whispered in his ear.

"What is that?" said deJuin.

"You are a believer now. That is the true name of Uctut and only believers may speak that word. Should an unbeliever say it aloud, the skies will darken and the clouds will fall. You may say it."

DeJuin was careful not to smile and spoke the word aloud. As he had suspected, the skies did not darken and the clouds did not fall, which Uncle Carl took as proof that deJuin believed truly and well.

Uncle Carl rose. "You are king. For thirty years I have waited for you, because you are blood of blood, soul of soul, of that ancient Actatl king of centuries ago. Now you must lead the family to victory."

DeJuin was surprised that he did not regard his uncle's words as foolish.

"We will do that, Uncle," he said.

"And we will avenge the desecration?"

"When we work all this out, Uctut will have all the hearts it ever wanted," deJuin said.

And that night, before he fell asleep, he said the secret name of Uctut again. And when the skies did not darken and the clouds did not fall, he knew.

He did not know if he was a believer, but he knew that the Actatl had at last gained a king who would lead them to glory.

Chapter Eight

When Jean Louis deJuin and his Uncle Carl arrived in New York, they went directly to a Fifth Avenue hotel where a battery of bellhops waited to handle their luggage, where they were not required to register, where the presidential suite had been vacated for them, and where the hotel manager gave Uncle Carl a large knowing wink, convincing deJuin that no matter what it might mean as a tradition and religion, the international brotherhood of Uctut followers had a great deal of secular clout.

"I had never realized the family was so extensive," deJuin said after he and Carl had dismissed the bellboys and sat in the drawing room of the large five-room suite.

"We are everywhere," said Uncle Carl. "You would have known if you had paid more attention when you were young." He smiled, more critical than mirthful.

"But I am here now," said deJuin, returning the smile.

"Yes, Jean Louis, and I am grateful for that and will indulge in no more recriminations, no matter how pleasant they may be."

"Recriminations are pleasant only for losers," deJuin said, "as an explanation to themselves of why their lives went wrong. You are not a loser and your life has not gone wrong. In fact, it will now go most extremely right, and so recriminations do not become you."

Then deJuin directed the older man to begin immediately to call in members of the family to speak to deJuin. "We must plan now better than we have ever planned before, and I must study our resources. I will be ready to speak to people in two hours."

He went into a bedroom and on a large oaken desk spread out papers from the alligator leather briefcase he had carried with him.

Before sitting down, he removed the jacket of his gray chalk-striped suit. He carefully undid his monogrammed French cuffs and turned his shirt sleeves up two precise folds. He undid his collar and carefully removed his black and red silk tie and hung it over a hanger with his jacket, which he placed in one of the large, oil-soaked cedar closets.

DeJuin clicked on the wood-framed fluorescent light and took the caps off two broad-tipped marking pens, one red and one black. The red was for writing down possibilities; the black was for crossing them out after he decided they would not work.

He held the red marker toward his lips and looked through the window at the early afternoon sun shining down on the busy street, then he fell upon the pile of blank white paper as if he were an eagle plummeting down onto a mouse that had the misfortune to wander across a patch of land that offered no cover.

When again he looked up, there was no sun. The sky was dark, and he realized afternoon had slipped away into evening.

The wastepaper basket was overflowing with crumpled sheets of paper. The top of the desk looked like the overflow from the wastebasket.

But one sheet was squared neatly in front of deJuin. On it was written one neat word, printed in red block capitals: INFILTRATE.

When he went back into the drawing room, a dozen men were there, sitting quietly. They were mostly middle-aged men, wearing business suits with vests buckled down by university chains, straight-legged pants, and the highly polished leather shoes favored by practical men who can afford any kind of shoe they wish and choose the same kind they grew up wearing.

All rose as he entered the room.

Uncle Carl rose too from his chair near the window.

"Gentlemen. Our king. Jean Louis deJuin."

The dozen men sank slowly to their knees.

DeJuin looked at Uncle Carl questioningly, as if

for the command that would bring the men to their feet. But Carl too had gone to his knees, his bowed head extended toward deJuin.

"The name of Uctut cannot be defiled," said de-Juin. "It is all holiness and beyond the dirtying touch of men. But for those who have tried, Uctut calls for sacrifice, and we of the Actatl shall provide that sacrifice. This I vow—this we all vow. On our honor and our lives." He paused. "Rise."

The men got slowly to their feet, their faces illuminated with an inner glow, and came forward to shake deJuin's hand and to introduce themselves.

DeJuin waited, then waved the men to seats on the couches and chairs in the room.

"Our first goal is to get close to these two, this American and the aged Oriental. From them we will move against their organization and expropriate its power. The question is, how do we infiltrate? How do we get close to these two men?"

He looked around the room. He had expected puzzled looks, but instead he found smiles that showed satisfaction. He looked to Uncle Carl.

Carl rose. "We have ways of getting to those two."

He smiled.

"Two ways," he said.

Chapter Nine

Remo carefully addressed the large trunk to an oil company operating in Nome, Alaska. By the time the trunk reached the company, it would be winter in Nome. The trunk would go into the warehouse, and not until summer would someone notice the funny smell and eventually the body of the Justice Department official. Who had almost caught Remo off guard. But in this business, "almost" meant flying to Nome in a trunk because you kept better till next summer.

"Return address, sir?" said the clerk at the railway station.

"Disneyworld, Florida," said Remo. The clerk said he had always wanted to go to the place and asked if Remo worked there, and Remo said he was president of the Mickey Mouse union.

"Mickey Mouse for short," said Remo. "Actually it's the International Brotherhood of Mickey Mice, Donald Ducks, Goofies, and Seven Dwarfs of America, AFL-CIO. That's dwarfs, not dwarves. We may go on strike next week over our mistreatment by cartoonists. Not enough lines."

"Oh," said the clerk suspiciously. But he nevertheless sent William Reddington III, assistant director, northern district, New York, on his Nome vacation with two loud pounds of a rubber stamp.

Reddington had been the strangest assault. He came padding in to Remo's hotel suite in a four-hundred-dollar blue striped suit with vest, a Phi Beta Kappa key, and light brown hair immaculately combed to casualness.

He was sorry to bother Remo at that hour, and he knew the tension everyone in the room must be suffering, but he had come to help.

Chiun was asleep in one of the bedrooms. Remo had not been sure the two women would be safe if he just turned them free after the slaughter at the museum, so he told them they must stay with him for a while. Valerie had started sobbing at that moment, and when Reddington arrived, she was still sobbing, staring straight ahead in a state of shock. Bobbi Delpheen watched the late late show, starring Tyrone Power as a handsome but destitute Italian nobleman. She had also watched the late show where Tyrone Power had starred as a handsome but destitute French nobleman. Power had died, Bobbi commented, while making

112

the greatest picture of his life—the story of a handsome but destitute Spanish nobleman.

Remo nodded for Reddington to enter.

"I'm from the Department of Justice," he said. "I hear you've been having some trouble."

"No trouble," said Remo, shrugging.

"*Whaaaaa,*" said Valerie.

"Are you all right, dear?" asked Reddington.

"Oh, my god," said Valerie. "A sane person. Thank God. Thank God. A sane human being." And her gentle sobs released in a heave of tears, and she stumbled to Reddington and cried into his shoulder as he patted her back.

"She's all right," said Remo. "You're all right, aren't you, Valerie?"

"Drop dead, you freaking animal," cried Valerie. "Keep him away from me," she said to Reddington.

"I think someone is trying to kill you," said Reddington. "And I don't even know your name."

"Albert Schweitzer," said Remo.

"He's lying. It's Remo something. I don't know the last name. He's a lunatic killer. You don't even see his hands move. He's murderous, brutal, cold, and sarcastic."

"I am not sarcastic," said Remo.

"Don't listen to that broad," called out Bobbi. "She doesn't even play tennis. She sits around and cries all day. She's a punk loser."

"Thank you," said Remo. Bobbi raised her right hand in an okay sign.

"He kills people with his hands and feet," said Valerie.

113

"I take it you're a karate master of some sort," said Reddington.

"No," said Remo, and in this he was honest. "I am not karate. Karate just focuses power."

"And you use it for self-defense?" Reddington asked.

"He uses it on anyone in sight," said Valerie.

"I haven't used it on you," said Remo.

"You will."

"Maybe," said Remo, imagining what Valerie would look like with a mouth removed from her face. It would be an improvement.

"As I said," Reddington explained, "I've come to help. But first I must see your weapons. Are your hands your only weapons?"

"No," Remo said. "Hands are just an extension of the weapon we all share. That's the difference between man and animals. Animals use their limbs; man uses his mind."

"Then you're an animal," said Valerie, creating a large wet spot of tears on Reddington's lapel.

"Just your body, then?" said Reddington musingly. He excused himself for backing away from Valerie Gardner, and she was the first to see the .45 caliber automatic come out of Reddington's neat pinstriped jacket. She realized she was between the gun and the lunatic behind her and all she said was "To hell with it." A man from the Justice Department was making her a shield in a shooting gallery. Her, Valerie Gardner, she had to go and meet the only US Attorney who doubled as a hit man.

"Go ahead and shoot the damned thing," she yelled.

"Come on, fella. Is this any way to act?" Remo said.

"Right," Valerie shrieked, wheeling from Reddington to Remo and back. "Right. That's the way to act. Shoot the damned thing. Get this homicidal maniac before he gets us all."

"Quiet," said Remo. "I'm going to get to you later." He smiled at Reddington. "We should sit and reason together," he said hopefully.

Reddington backed off a step, beyond the reach of Remo's arm and leg, so he could not be disarmed by a sudden move.

"There is nothing to discuss," he said, "with one who has laid hands on the high priests of Uctut."

"What priests?" said Remo. "Those loonies who were trying to open my chest without a key?"

"Shoot," shrieked Valerie. "Shoot."

Reddington ignored her. His eyes seemed fixed on Remo with a cold stare, his lids too icy to blink.

"Through the ages, there has been Uctut," he said to Remo. "And there have been those of us who have defended him against the desecrators who would do our God evil."

"Wait a minute," Remo said. "You were the guy standing guard outside the congressman's office when he got it, weren't you?"

"Yes. And I lifted his heart from his chest myself," Reddington said.

Remo nodded. "I thought so. I wondered how a flock of two-hundred-pound canaries could have sneaked past a guard."

"And now it is your turn," Reddington said.

115

"Nixon made me do it," Remo said.

"It is past excuses."

"Bobby Kennedy?" Remo offered. "Jack Kennedy? J. Edgar Hoover?"

"It will not do," said Reddington.

"Don't say I didn't try," Remo said.

Reddington backed up another step.

"Shoot, will you?" yelled Valerie. "Off this violent lunatic."

Reddington held the gun professionally, near his right hip. This was the way taught by the Justice Department to prevent its men from being disarmed by someone just reaching out and slapping or kicking the gun away.

But for every counter there is a counter, and when Remo went into a sudden move to Reddington's left, Reddington found that the gun could not home in on Remo as it should because Reddington's own hip was in the way. He wheeled to his left to keep the gun on Remo, but when he turned, Remo was not there anymore. He turned again, this time to the rear, and there he found Remo, but he had no chance to celebrate his discovery with a one-gun salute because the gun, still held properly against his hip, was pushed back above the hip, through his side, past his abdominal cavity, and into the center of Reddington's right kidney, where it came to rest.

Reddington fell, eyes still iced over.

"Killer! Killer!," Valerie shrieked.

"Quiet," Remo said. "You're going to get yours."

Bobbie looked up from the television set. "Do it

now," she said. "Get rid of this twit and let's go out and hit a few. There's an all-night court over on the East Side. Clay court too. I don't like playing on hard surfaces. And you don't get a true bounce on grass. Unless you've got a big serve. If you've got a big serve, then I'd probably give you a better game on grass because it'd slow down your serve."

"I don't play tennis," Remo said.

"That's revolting," Bobbi said. "This one was right. He should have killed you."

"Quiet. Both of you," Remo said. "I'm trying to think."

"This should be good," Valerie said.

"Think about taking up tennis," Bobbi said.

Remo decided instead to think about how much he remembered the boy scout adviser who had come to the orphanage in Newark to start a scout troop. All the orphans over twelve, Remo included, had joined because the nuns had ordered them to. That had lasted only until the nuns found out that the scoutmaster was teaching the boys how to start fires with flint and steel, and three mattress fires in an old wooden building with a flash point somewhat lower than butane gas convinced the nuns to evict the boy scouts and think about affiliation with a 4-H club.

Remo had never learned how to build a fire with flint and steel. He hadn't been able to steal a lump of flint from any of the other boys, and the little pieces that came in cigarette lighters were too small to get a good grip on.

But Remo had learned knots. The scoutmaster

had been a whiz on knots. Bowlines and sheep-shanks and clove hitches. Square knots. Right over left and left over right. Reno thought about those knots. Bowlines were best, he decided. The knot was designed for tying together two differ-ent thicknesses of rope and this would come in very handy when he trussed up Bobbi and Valerie with the thick pieces of drapery rope and the thin cord from the venetian blinds.

"We'll scream for help," Valerie threatened.

"You do that and I'll tie a sheepshank on you, too," said Remo.

He tied up Valerie with bowlines. He tied an-other drapery cord over her mouth in a gag and fastened it with a clove hitch. It came loose so he changed it to a square knot tied tightly behind her neck.

"You?" he said to Bobbi.

"Actually I was planning to be quiet," she said.

"Good," said Remo, tying her up but leaving off the gag. "The old gentleman is sleeping inside. If you're unlucky enough to wake him up before he chooses to rise, it's going to be game, set, and match point for you, kid."

"I understand," she said, but Remo wasn't lis-tening. He was wondering what had gone wrong with the clove hitch he had tried to use to tie Val-erie's mouth. He tried it again when he packaged Reddington for his Alaskan sabbatical and was pleased when the knots held very tightly.

It gave him a warm feeling of accomplishment that he kept all the way to the railway station, where he mailed Reddington to Alaska, and on a

118

long all-night walk through Central Park, where he fed a mugger to the ducks, and all the way back to his hotel suite, when he found out that Bobbi was gone.

She had been kidnapped.

Chapter Ten

Chiun was sitting in the center of the floor watching television. Valerie was trussed in a corner of the room.

"Where's Bobbi?" Remo said.

Valerie mumbled through her gag. *"Gree-grawkgra. Neargh, graw, graw."*

"Shut up," said Remo. "Chiun, where's Bobbi?"

Chiun did not turn. He raised a hand over his head as if in dismissal.

Remo sighed and reluctantly started to untie the gag from Valerie's mouth. It was triple-knotted, and the square knots he had used had given way to some other kind of knot Remo had never seen before. His fingers had to pick tightly at the strands of drapery sash before he got the gag off.

"He did it, he did it," said Valerie. She nodded at Chiun.

"*Shhhhh,*" Chiun hissed

"Shut up," Remo said to Valerie. "Where's Bobbi?"

"They came for her. Three men in the yellow feathered robes. I tried to tell him, but he tied me up again. Pig!" she shouted across the room at Chiun.

"Kid, do yourself a favor and knock that off," Remo said.

A commercial came on the television. For the next two minutes and five seconds, Remo had Chiun to himself.

"Chiun, did you see them take Bobbi?"

"If you mean was I awakened from my few golden moments of rest by uncalled for intrusions, yes. If you mean when I came out here, did this disciple of the open mouth verbally abuse me with her noise, yes. If you mean—"

"I mean did you see the three men take the other girl away?"

"If you mean, did I see three creatures who looked like the big bird on the children's program, yes. I laughed, they were so funny."

"And you just let them go?" Remo said.

"This one was making enough noise for two persons, even through the gag that was so ineptly tied. I did not need a second female here to make even more noise. If they had promised to come back for this one, I would have put her outside

121

the door to await them, as if she were an empty bottle of milk."

"Dammit, Chiun. Those were the people I wanted. We've been looking for them. What do you think we've had these girls here for? In the hope that those Indians would come to us."

"Correction. You have been looking for those people. I have carefully avoided looking for them."

"That girl's going to be killed. I hope you're proud of yourself."

"There are too many tennis players in the world already."

"She's going to have her heart cut out."

"Perhaps they will settle for her tongue."

"That's right. Make fun," Valerie shrieked. "You miserable old man."

Chiun turned around and looked behind him.

"Who is she talking to?" he asked Remo.

"Ignore her."

"I try to. I came out of my room and I was so kind as to untie her mouth. That proves that even the Master is not beyond error. The noise that came out. So I retied her."

"And you just let those three yellow ostriches take Bobbi away?"

"I was getting tired of talking about tennis," said Chiun. "It is a stupid game anyway."

The commercial ended, and he turned his face away from Remo and back toward the television set, where Dr. Rance McMasters was congratulating Mrs. Wendell Waterman on her elevation to acting chairman of the Silver City Bicentennial Commission, a post she was hastily named to when the permanent chairman, Mrs. Ferd Delanettes, contracted a terminal case of syphilis, given her by Dr. Rance McMasters, who was now talking softly to Mrs. Waterman, preparatory to giving her a dose of her own in the twenty-three hours and thirty minutes between the end of this day's episode and the start of tomorrow's.

"Is there any chance, any slight chance," Remo asked Valerie, "that while those dingdongs were here, you kept your mouth shut long enough to hear anything they said?"

"I heard every word, freak," she said.

"Give me a few."

"The biggest one—"

"Did you ever see any of them before?" Remo asked.

"What a stupid question!" Valerie said. "How many people do you see in New York wearing yellow feathers?"

"More this year than last. They weren't born with feathers, you know. Underneath there are men. They look like men. Did you recognize any of them?"

"No."

"Okay, what'd they say?"

"The biggest one said, 'Miss Delpheen?' and she nodded, and he said, 'You are coming with us.' "

"And what happened?"

"They untied her and—"

"Did she say anything?"

"No. What could she say?"

"I'll bet you could have thought of something. What else?"

"Then they took her by the hands and walked

123

out the door. That one—" She nodded to Chiun. "He came out of the bedroom. He saw them, but instead of trying to stop them, he went and turned on the television set. They left. I tried to call him, and he untied my mouth, but when I told him that she had been kidnapped, he tied my mouth again."

"Good for him," said Remo. "So you don't know where they went?"

"No," said Valerie. "Are you going to untie me?"

"I'm going to sleep on it," Remo said.

"They went to the Edgemont Mansion in Englewood, wherever that is," Chiun said softly without turning from the television.

"How do you know that?" Remo asked.

"I heard them, of course. How else would I know that? Be quiet now."

"Englewood's in New Jersey," Remo said.

"Then you will probably still find it there," Chiun said. "Silence."

"Finish it up," Remo said. "Then put on your tape machine. You're coming with me."

"Of course. Order me around."

"Why not? It's all your fault," said Remo.

Chiun refused to answer. He fastened his gaze onto the small color television screen.

Remo went to the telephone. His first call to the private line in Smith's office drew a screeching whistle that indicated he had dialed wrong. After two more tries resulted in the same response, he decided the telephone had been disconnected.

On a chance, he called a private number that

rang on the desk of Smith's secretary in his outer office.

The telephone rang eight times before it was picked up and the familiar voice answered.

"Hello?"

"Smitty, how are you?"

"Remo—"

Remo saw Valerie watching him. "Just a minute," he said.

He picked up Valerie by her still-bound legs.

"What are you doing, swine?"

"Quiet," said Remo. He put her in a clothes closet and shut the door.

"Bitch. Bastard. Rotten bastard," she yelled, but the heavy door muffled the noise and Remo nodded with satisfaction as he picked up the telephone.

"Yeah, Smitty, sorry."

"Anything to report?" Smith asked.

"Just for once," Remo said, "couldn't you say something pleasant? Like 'hello' and 'how are you'? Couldn't you do that just for once?"

"Hello, Remo. How are you?"

"I don't want to talk to you," Remo said. "I just decided I don't want you to be my friend."

"All right, then," said Smith. "With that out of the way, have you anything to report?"

"Yes. The girl Bobbi Delpheen has been grabbed by those Indians."

"Where did this happen?"

"In my hotel room."

"And you let it happen?"

"I wasn't here."

"And Chiun?" asked Smith.

"He was busy. He was turning on his television set."

"Wonderful," said Smith dryly. "Everything's coming down around our ears, and I'm dealing with an absentee and a soap opera freak."

"Yeah, well, just calm yourself down. As it happens, we have a lead. A very good lead, and now I don't think I'm going to tell you about it."

"Now or never," said Smith and allowed himself a little chuckle that sounded like a bubble escaping from a pan of boiling vinegar.

"What does that mean?"

"I've finished dismantling this place now. There are too many federal agents around and we're just too vulnerable. We're closing down for a while."

"How will I reach you?"

"I've told my wife we're going on vacation. We've found a little place near Seboomook Mountain in Maine. This will be the number there." He gave Remo a number which Remo remembered automatically by scratching it into the varnish of the table with his right thumbnail.

"Do you have it?"

"I've got it," Remo said.

"It's odd for you to remember something first try," Smith said.

"I didn't call so you could bitch about my memory."

"No, of course not." Smith seemed to want to say more, but no more words came.

"How long are you going to be up there?" Remo asked.

"I don't know," Smith said. "If it looks like

people are getting too close and that the organization might be exposed, well . . . we might just stay there."

Smith spoke slowly, almost offhandedly, but Remo knew what he meant. If Smith and his wife "stayed there," it would be because dead men did not move, and Smith would choose death before risking exposure of the secret organization to which he had devoted more than ten years.

Remo wondered if he would ever be able to look forward to death with Smith's calmness, a calmness born of knowing he had done his job well.

Remo said, "I don't want you staying up there too long. You may get to like the idea of vacations. You might retire."

"Would it bother you?"

"Who'd pay off my expense accounts? My Texaco card?"

"Remo, what is that noise?"

"That's Valerie," Remo said. "She's in a closet, don't worry about her."

"She's the woman from the museum?"

"Right. Don't worry about her. When are you going to Maine?"

"I was just leaving."

"Have fun. If you want to know where the skiing's good, I know a great guidebook."

"Oh, really?" said Smith.

"Right," said Remo. "It tells you all about the illimitable skills and the indomitable courage of the author. It tells you all about the politics of the downslope trade and rips the mask of hypocrisy off the faces of the ski resort owners."

"I'll be at Seboomook Mountain. How's the skiing there?"

"Who knows?" Remo said. "The book doesn't get into things like that."

After hanging up, Remo gave Valerie her choice of options. She could go with them to the Edgemont Estate or she could stay tied up in the closet. If she were anyone else, there might have been a third option. She could be set free on the condition that she keep her mouth shut and not tell anybody anything.

He paused. Twice, he thought. Twice in five minutes he had worried about someone else's life. He savored the emotion before deciding he did not like it.

For her part, Valerie decided to go with Remo and Chiun, working on the assumption that she could never escape from a closet, but if she were outside with them, she might be able to slip away.

Or, at least, yell loud and long for a cop.

Jean Louis deJuin smoked a Gauloise cigarette in a long ebony filter that tried manfully but unsuccessfully to hide the fact that Gauloise cigarettes tasted like burned coffee grounds. He looked through the sheer draperies from the third floor window of the red brick mansion out onto the grounds between the building and the road beyond.

Uncle Carl stood alongside deJuin's red leather, high-backed chair and watched with him. DeJuin casually flicked ashes from his cigarette onto the highly polished wood parquet floors that had been set in place, individual piece by individual piece, back in a day when wood was something that craftsmen used, and not just a temporary stop on the road to the discovery of plastic.

"It was too bad about Reddington," Uncle Carl said.

DeJuin shrugged. "It was not unpredictable; still it was worth the attempt. Today we try again. All we need is one of those two men, and from him we can learn the secrets of the organization he works for. Do we have people looking through their rooms?"

"Yes, Jean Louis. As soon as they left, our men went up to look through the rooms. They will call if they find anything."

"Good. And the computers in Paris are analyzing the various capacities of American computer systems. If that secret organization is, as it must be, tied tightly into a computer system, our own computers will tell us where."

He looked up at Carl and smiled. "So there is nothing to do but enjoy the day's sport."

DeJuin snuffed his cigarette out on the floor and leaned forward to look through the open window. Three stories below him, twelve-foot-high hedges crisscrossed each other at sharp right angles, in the form of a geometric maze covering almost an acre.

Eliot Jansen Edgemont, who built the estate, had been an eccentric who made a fortune out of jokes and games, and during the twenties, half of America's families had owned one Edgemont game or another, back in the days before America had been mesmerized into thinking that sitting next to each other and sharing a communal stare at the photoelectric tube constituted a rich and full family life.

He invented his first game at age twenty-two. When no game manufacturer would buy it, he himself produced and sold the game to department stores. At twenty-six he was wealthy. At thirty he was "America's Puzzle Master," spinning out from his fertile mind game after game, all of them bearing the Edgemont emblem, a large block **E** set into the middle of a geometric maze.

For the maze had been the linchpin of Edgemont's success. While his early games had been successful, the first that had swept America in a craze had been a board game built around a maze. It was inevitable that the maze motif be built into Edgemont's life, and when he built his estate in Englewood, New Jersey, he copied a European idea for a maze of hedges on the grounds. Life Magazine had done a full color spread on it once: "The Mysterious Mansion of America's Puzzle King."

The story did not mention any of the more unusual aspects of Eliot Jansen Edgemont's life. Most specifically it did not mention the orgies that took place in the maze that separated the house from the road.

Then, on one fine summer day in the late 1940's, two male guests caught the same girl in the maze at the same time, and in the resulting argument over property rights, one of the men was killed.

The scandal could not be hushed up, and various legions aimed at preserving America from the godless hordes organized boycotts of Edgemont products. The puzzle and home game business had been on the downs anyway, slowly being destroyed by America's new toy, television, and so the old man took his games and went home.

He sold his business and retired to Europe, where people were more broad-minded, and he died there in the mid 1960's of a stroke suffered while tupping a fifteen-year-old girl in a haymow. It took the girl six minutes to realize he was dead.

She told police that Edgemont said something before he died, but she could not hear the word clearly. Even if she had, she would not have been able to repeat it, for it was the secret name of the stone god Uctut.

For Edgemont had been an Actatl.

In the disposition of his estate, the mansion in Englewood passed into the hands of a corporation that was controlled by the tribe.

It was usually seen only by workmen who kept the hedges trimmed and the buildings in good repair, except on days like this, when the Actatl needed a place to conduct some business.

Today there were no workmen on the grounds, and as Jean Louis deJuin looked down into the center of the maze that covered more than an acre, he smiled in satisfaction.

Everything was going very well.

He looked up as a blue Ford pulled up outside the spike-topped high metal gates two hundred yards from the house. Raising field glasses to his eyes, he watched as Remo, Chiun, and Valerie got out of the car. The two men, he thought, did not really look impressive. Except for the thick wrists on the white man, neither showed any indication of special physical prowess. But he remembered that the white man had gone through some of the Actatl's best warriors like a Saracen blade through flan, and he did not make judgments on appearances anyway.

The gate to the estate had been locked at de-Juin's order with a new heavy-duty chain and padlock. As he watched, deJuin saw the padlock and chain fall away under the hands of the Oriental as if they were paper.

Then the two men and the woman were walking between the twelve-foot-high walls of hedge toward the house, which sat on a small rise two hundred yards away. The alley through which they walked was about six feet wide.

DeJuin moved back from the window, set down his binoculars, and glanced down into the main body of the maze. Everything was ready.

The three people had reached the end of the hedge-lined walkway. A wall of hedge prevented their going farther ahead and they must choose now to turn left into the maze or go back. The Oriental looked behind them at the gate. He spoke, but deJuin could not hear the words.

The white man shook his head no, grabbed the girl roughly by the elbow, and turned left. The Oriental followed slowly.

Then they were into the maze, turning right, turning left, the white man leading the way, following the small paths down blind alleys, then turning back, slowly, steadily working their way toward the center.

The telephone on the floor next to deJuin

buzzed slightly, and he nodded for Uncle Carl to answer it.

He stared at the three, and when they were deep in the heart of the labyrinth, deJuin pulled the sheer curtain back a few inches and leaned forward toward the open window.

He made a small gesture with his hand, then leaned onto the windowsill to watch. This was going to be interesting.

"Why are we here?" Chiun demanded. "Why are we in this place of many turns?"

"Because we are going to that house to get Bobbi back. Remember her? You let them take her because you were busy watching your television shows?"

"That's right," said Chiun. "Blame it on me. Blame everything on me. It's all right. I'm used to it."

"Stop carping and—"

"So it's carp again, is it?" said Chiun.

"Stop complaining," said Remo, holding Valerie tightly by her elbow, "and help me find our way to the house. I'm getting confused in here."

"You were confused before you got here," said Chiun. "You have always been confused."

"Right, right, right. You win. Now will you help me get to the house?"

"We could go over the hedges," Chiun suggested.

"Not with this one," Remo said, nodding toward Valerie.

"Or through them," Chiun said.

"She'd get cut. Then she'd probably start yelling. I couldn't take it if her mouth was going."

Remo reached a blank wall of hedge. Another dead end.

"Dammit," he said.

"If we cannot go through or over," Chiun said, "there is only one thing to do."

"Which is . . ."

"Find our way through this growth."

"That's what I'm trying to do," Remo said.

"Actually it is a simple little toy," Chiun said. "Once there was a master, this was many years ago in what you would call the time of the pharaohs, and while in the land of the Egyptians, oh, to what a test he was put with one of these labyrinths and it was only his—"

"Please, Chiun, no puff pieces for great masters you have known and loved. Bottom line. Do you know how to get through this thing?"

"Of course. Each master is privileged to share the learnings of all the masters who have gone before."

"And?"

"And what?" asked Chiun.

"And how the hell do we get through this thing?"

"Oh." Chiun sighed. "Put out your right hand and touch the wall of hedge."

Remo touched the spiny green bush. "Now what?"

"Just move forward. Be sure your hand is against a wall at all times. Follow it around corners, into dead ends, everywhere it takes you. You must eventually find the exit."

Remo looked at Chiun with narrowed eyes. "Are you sure this will work?"

"Yes."

"Why didn't you tell me before?"

"I thought you wanted to do it your way. Running down alleys until they disappeared and then yelling at the plants. I did not know you wanted to do this efficiently. It has never been one of the things you are most interested in."

"No more talk. Let's get to the house." Remo moved away at a trot, keeping Valerie close to his left side, his right hand extended, fingertips on the hedge wall.

Chiun moved along after them, seeming only to amble, but staying just a step behind.

"They found a telephone number in the room," Uncle Carl hissed to deJuin. "It is a number in the state of Maine for a Dr. Harold Smith."

"Smith?" mused deJuin, still staring into the maze. "Call Paris and have our computer run the name of Smith through its memories." He smiled as he watched Remo reach out his hand and touch the hedge. DeJuin had nodded. So the secrets of a maze were no secret to the old man.

DeJuin raised his hand slightly in a small gesture, careful not to call attention to himself.

"And let the fun begin," he said.

"There is someone in that window, Remo," Chiun said.

"I know. I saw."

"Two persons," Chiun said. "One young, one old." He was interrupted as a voice rang out over the maze. It echoed and seemed to come from all around them.

"Help. Help." And then there was a scream.

"That's Bobbi," Remo said.

"Yes," said Chiun. "The voice came from over there." He pointed at the wall of the hedges, in the general pilot's direction of ten o'clock.

Remo broke away into a run. He let Valerie go. She was unsure of herself, but suspecting she was safer with Remo than away from him, she ran after him.

As deJuin watched from the window, he saw something that even later he would find difficult to believe.

The old Oriental did not run after the white man. He looked around him, then raced into the hedge to his left. DeJuin winced. He could imagine what the prickers and thorns were doing to the old man's flesh. Then the old man was in the passageway on the other side of the hedge, moving across the six feet of gravel and charging again into another of the five-foot-thick growths of shrubs. And then he was through that, too.

"Help, Remo, help," Bobbi's voice came again.

When the maze was built, it had been designed around a small central court, and Bobbi Delpheen was there. She was tied to a high marble bench. Her tennis shirt had been ripped open and her bare breasts were exposed.

Behind her stood two men wearing the yellow feather robes. One held a wedge of stone, its two edges chipped into a knife blade.

They stood looking down at her, and then they looked up. Coming through the hedge directly facing them was a small Oriental in a golden robe.

"Hold," he called. His voice rang out like a whipcrack.

The men froze in position momentarily, then both turned and fled into one of the pathways leading away from the central court. Chiun moved to the side of the girl, whose arms and legs were tied to the corners of the bench.

"Are you all right?"

"Yes," Bobbi said. Her lips trembled as she spoke.

She looked up at Chiun then past him as Remo suddenly raced into the clearing. A few paces behind him came Valerie.

Chiun flicked at the ropes binding Bobbi's wrists and ankles and they fell away under his fingernails.

"Is she all right?" Remo asked.

"No thanks to you," Chiun said. "It's all right that I have to do everything around here."

"What happened?" Remo asked.

"She was here. The feathered men fled as the Master approached," Chiun said.

"Why didn't you chase them?" Remo asked.

"Why didn't you?"

"I wasn't here."

"That was not my fault," Chiun said.

Bobbi stood up from the marble slab that served as a bench. Her tennis shirt hung open and her bosom jutted forward.

Oblivious to that, she rubbed her wrists, which were red and chafed.

"You'll never be a tennis player," Remo said.

Bobbi looked up, startled. "Why not?"

"Too much between you and your backhand."

"Cover yourself up. That's disgusting," Valerie shrieked—again proving that beauty is in the eye of the beholder and that "disgusting" is a 38-C being viewed by a 34-B.

Bobbi looked down at herself as if at a stranger, then took a deep breath before pulling her shirt closed and tucking the ends into the waistband of her tennis shorts.

"Did they hurt you?" Remo asked.

"No. But they ... they were going to cut my heart out." The last words came out in a gush, as if speaking them slowly would have been impossible, but there was less horror in haste.

Remo glanced toward the house. "Chiun, you get these girls out of here. I'm going after those two canaries."

"Girls?" shouted Valerie. "Girls? Girls? That's patronizing."

Remo raised his left index finger in a caution. "You've been a very good girl up until now," he said. "Now if you don't want your jaw patronized by my fist, you'll shut off that perpetual motion machine you call a mouth. Chiun, I'll meet you at the car."

Behind him, deJuin heard the two men in feathered robes enter the room. Without looking, he waved them forward to the window. "This will be good now," he said.

The four men leaned forward to watch.

"Be careful," Chiun said to Remo.

"You got it," Remo said.

He turned, but before he could take a step

138

away, the corridors of the maze resounded with a deep angry baying. The sound was answered by another howl. And another.

"Oh, my god," said Valerie. "There are animals here."

"Three," said Chiun to Remo. "Large."

The baying changed now into angry excited barks that moved closer.

"Take the girls, Chiun. I'll watch the rear."

Chiun nodded. "When you leave," he said, "place your left hand against the wall. It will bring you back the way you came."

"I know that," said Remo, who did not know that.

Chiun led the girls away down one of the gravel paths leading from the central courtyard.

The barking was louder now, growing more frenzied. Remo watched as Chiun and the two women hurried down the passageway, then turned left and vanished from sight.

Along one of the paths to the right, Remo caught his first glimpse. It was a Doberman Pinscher, black, brown, and ugly. His eyes glinted savagely, almost taking on a blood-red glow, as he saw Remo standing in front of the marble slab bench. Behind him came two more Dobermans, big dogs, one hundred pounds each of muscle and teeth that glistened white and deadly, like miniature railroad spikes covered with dental enamel.

When they all saw Remo, they drove forward even faster, each trying to be first to get to the prize. Remo watched them coming, the most savage of all dogs, a breed created by intermingling other dogs selected for their size, their strength, and their savagery.

They moved together now in a straight line, coming at Remo shoulder to shoulder, like three tines of a deadly pitchfork.

Remo leaned back against the marble slab.

"Here, poochie, poochie, poochie," he called.

Remo moved a few feet farther to his right, away from the path Chiun and the women had taken. He did not want the dogs to be diverted from him and go off chasing a random smell.

With one final growl delivered almost in unison, the three Dobermans moved into the clearing. They crossed the space between themselves and Remo in just two giant strides, and then they were in the air, their muzzles close together, their hindquarters separated, looking like deadly feathers attached to an invisible dart.

Their open jaws all went for Remo's throat.

He paused until the final instant, then moved down under the three soaring dogs.

He sent the center one up over his head with his shoulder. The dog did a slow, almost lazy flip in the air and landed on its back on the marble slab with a splat. He yelped once, softly, then slid off onto the gravel on the far side.

Remo took out the dog on the right with an upward thrust of the bent knuckle of his right middle finger. He had never struck a dog before, and he was surprised at how much a dog's belly felt like a man's belly.

The results of the stroke were the same, too, as with a man. The dog dropped dead at Remo's feet.

The Doberman on the left missed Remo, hit the

140

marble slab, skidded on its paws, fell off the slab, scrambled to its feet again, and turned back with a snarl toward Remo, who was backing away.

He came through the air at Remo just as Remo decided he did not like killing dogs, even Dobermans who would gladly kill him just to keep their teeth cavity-free.

As the dog's massive head turned to the left so its powerful open jaws could encircle Remo's throat, Remo leaned back, pulling his neck away, and the jaws closed harmlessly with a loud click as tooth surface contacted tooth surface.

Remo reached down and with his left hand dislocated the beast's right front leg. The dog yelped and hit the ground. Remo walked away.

The dog got up on three feet, and dragging its dislocated leg, ran toward Remo again. Remo heard the injured limb scudding through the white gravel. He turned as the dog growled and reared up on its two hind legs, trying to bite him.

He slapped the big dog's wettish nose with his left hand and dislocated the other front leg with his right hand. This time, when the dog hit the ground, it stayed there, whining and whimpering.

In the window high above Remo, deJuin moved back from the curtain. He felt the feathers of the two men on his sides brush his face. "Marvelous," he said softly.

Below, as if he had heard the Frenchman, Remo turned, remembering the men who had been watching from the window, and he pointed an index finger as if to say "you're next."

Then he darted up one of the paths leading away from the central courtyard to the house.

141

Forty yards away from Remo, but separated by many twists and turns, Chiun had heard the dogs' frenzied barking and yelping and then the screeches and then the silence.

"It is well," he said, continuing to shuffle forward with the two women.

He stopped suddenly short and spread his arms to prevent the two women from lurching forward. The women bumped into his thin arms, extended outward from his sides. Each let out an "oof" as if they had walked stomach first into an iron guardrail.

Valerie got her breath back first. "Why are we stopped? Let's get out of here." She looked to Bobbi for agreement, but the buxom blonde stood silent, still apparently shaken from her near miss cardiectomy on the marble slab.

"We will wait for Remo," Chiun said.

From the window, Jean Louis deJuin saw the old Korean stop. He saw Remo now, atop the hedges, racing along them as if they were a paved road, coming toward the house, and he shouted, "Withdraw." He and Uncle Carl and the two men in feathered robes fled from the window.

Ten seconds later Remo came through the open window in a rolling vault from the top of the tightly packed hedges.

The room was empty.

Remo went out into the hall and searched each room.

"Come out, come out, wherever you are," he called.

But all the rooms were empty. Back in the room he had first entered, Remo found a yellow

142

feather on the floor and consoled himself with the thought that even if he didn't find the men, the mange might yet carry them off.

He stuck the long feather into the hair over his right ear, like a plume, then dove through the window with a cry of "Excelsior!"

He turned a slow loop in the air, landed on his feet atop the hedge, and ran across the interstices of it toward where he saw Chiun and the two women up ahead.

DeJuin waited a few moments, then pressed the button which opened the wall panel in the room where they had been sitting. He and the other men stepped out from the secret room, and deJuin motioned to them for silence as they moved toward the window, standing alongside it, peering through the side of the curtain.

He saw Remo stop atop the hedges twelve feet above where Chiun and the two women still stood.

"Hey, Little Father," said Remo.

"What are you doing up there?" Chiun asked. "Why are you wearing that feather?"

"I thought it was kind of dashing," Remo said. "Why aren't you at the car?"

"There is a boomer down here," Chiun said.

Remo looked down. "Where is it? I don't see it."

"It is here. A wire buried under the stones. I saw the thin upraised line of rocks. I would not expect you to see it, particularly when your feathers get in your eyes. How fortunate that it was me leading these young people and not you."

"Yeah? Who took care of the dogs?" Remo asked. "Who always does all the dirty work?"

143

"Who is better qualified for dirty work?" Chiun asked. He liked that so he repeated it with a little chuckle. "Who is better qualified? Heh, heh."

"Where's the bomb?" said Remo, pulling the yellow feather from his hair and dropping it into the hedge.

"Right here," Chiun said. He pointed to a spot on the ground. "Heh, heh. Who is better qualified? Heh, heh."

"I ought to leave you there," Remo said.

As deJuin watched from the window, he saw Remo drop lightly from the top of the hedge to the outside of the tall iron fence that bordered one side of it. He could not see it, but he heard metal screeching as Remo separated the bars of the fence. A moment later he saw Remo stand up and he heard his voice.

"Okay, Little Father, it's disconnected."

"That means that it is safe?"

"Safe. I guarantee it."

"Say your final prayers," Chiun told the two women. "The white one guarantees your safety." But he led the two women past the wire imbedded under the gravel and toward the gate at the end of the pathway.

Remo walked along on the outside of the hedge.

"I have been thinking," Chiun said through the hedge to Remo.

"It's about time," Remo said. "Heh, heh. It's about time. Heh, heh."

"Listen to him," Chiun told the two women. "A child. Amused by a child's joke."

Which took all the fun out of it for Remo, and

he said to Chiun: "What were you thinking about?"

"About the Master that I told you about, who went to far off places and new worlds and was not fully believed."

"What about him?" Remo asked.

"I am still thinking," Chiun said and would say no more.

DeJuin watched as the old Oriental led the two women through the open gate. Remo had trotted along outside the fence, and then vaulted the twelve-foot-high fence with no more effort than if it had been the low right field handrail in Yankee Stadium.

They started to get into the car, but then the old man turned around, looked at the house, and began to speak words that gave deJuin an unexplained chill.

"May your ears burn as fire," Chiun called toward the house in a voice suddenly strong.

"May they feel the tingle of cold and then snap as glass. The House of Sinanju tells you that you will tear off your eyelids to feed your eyes to the eagles of the sky. And then you will shrink until you are eaten by the mice of the fields.

"All this, I, Master of Sinanju, tell you. Be fearful."

And then the old man stared at the window, and deJuin, even concealed by the curtain, felt as if those hazel eyes were burning into his. Then the old man entered the blue Ford and the American drove off.

DeJuin turned to the other men in the room, whose faces had turned white.

"What is it?" he said to Uncle Carl.

"It is an ancient curse, from the people of the plumed serpent in our land. It is very strong magic."

"Nonsense," said deJuin, who did not really feel such confidence. He had begun to speak again when the phone tingled softly at his feet.

He picked up the instrument and listened. Slowly his features relaxed and he smiled. *"Merci,"* he finally said and hung up.

"You have learned something?" asked Uncle Carl.

"Yes," said deJuin. "We will leave these two alone. We no longer need them to bring us to their leader. The computers never fail."

"The computers?" asked Carl.

"Yes. The name our kinsmen learned in the hotel room. Harold Smith. Well, Dr. Harold Smith is head of a sanitarium near here called Folcroft. And it has a computer system with access to most of the major computers in this country."

"And that means?" asked Uncle Carl.

"That means that this Dr. Smith is the head of the organization which employs these two assassins. And now that we know that, we will leave these two alone. We do not need them to attain our goals of power for the Actatl."

"But that leaves us always vulnerable," Carl protested.

DeJuin shook his head and let a slow smile take over his face.

"No. These two men are the arms. Strong and mighty arms, but only arms nevertheless. We will cut off the head of this secret organization. And

146

without the head, the arms are useless. So our trap did not work, but we have won anyway."

He kept his smile, and it spread infectiously to the other three men. DeJuin looked out into the maze at the central court, where two dogs lay dead and the third Doberman lay whimpering with two dislocated front legs.

Behind him, he heard the men say in unison: "You are king. You are king."

He turned. "That is true." And to one of the feather-wearing men, he said: "Go out and kill that dog."

In the car leaving the Edgemont Estate, Remo asked Chiun: "What was that all about? Eagles and mice and eyeballs of glass?"

"I thought of what that long-ago Master wrote in the histories. He said it was a powerful curse among the people he had visited."

"You don't even know, though, if these are the same people," Remo said.

Chiun formed his fingers into a delicate steeple. "Ah," he said. "But if it is, they will have sleepless nights."

Remo shrugged. When he glanced in the rearview mirror, Valerie was sitting sullenly against the door on the right side, but Bobbi Delpheen's face was white and drawn. She had really been frightened, Remo realized.

Chapter Eleven

The police found Joey 172 that night under a railroad bridge in the Bronx.

They did not find his heart.

There was almost a witness to the killing, who said that he was walking beneath the bridge when he heard a scuffle and a groan. He coughed and the sound stopped, and then he left. He came back fifteen minutes later and found Joey 172's body.

Alongside his body was a small note on the pavement, apparently written in his own blood by Joey 172. It said "Maine next." Police believed that in the brief reprieve Joey 172 got by the presence of the passerby, he had written this message on the ground.

This was all reported the next day by the *Post*, which Remo read.

That the *Post* took the message "Maine next" to mean that the killing was the work of a right wing lunatic fringe whose next mission was to go to Maine and make sure that the fascists won the Presidential election there was immaterial.

That the *Post* first and alone promulgated this theory on page one, and by page twenty-four, the editorial page, had promoted it to the status of fact by referring to it in an editorial entitled "Heartless in America" did not impress Remo at all.

What impressed him was the contents of the message. "Maine next."

What else could it mean but Dr. Harold Smith?

Throughout the Actatl tribe, the word had flashed on the death of Joey 172: The despoiler of the great stone Uctut is no more.

Another message flashed through, too. Soon the Actatl would be hidden no more; their proud historical traditions would no longer be kept secret by fear of annihilation and reprisal.

Soon the Actatl and their god Uctut, of the secret name, would stand high among the peoples of the world, proud and noble, for even now the leaders of the family were planning to humble a secret organization of the United States.

DeJuin sat in his hotel suite and gathered to him the bravest of the Actatl. They planned their trip. And when Uncle Carl insisted upon going, deJuin made no argument. The old man, he felt, deserved to be in on the moment of glory.

Chapter Twelve

Before Remo could pick up the telephone to call Dr. Harold Smith, the phone rang.

It was uncanny, Remo thought, how Smith sometimes seemed to be able, across many miles, to read Remo's mind and call just when Remo wanted to speak to him. But Smith had a far stronger track record of calling when Remo did not wish to speak to him, which was most of the time.

The phone rang again.

"Answer the instrument," Chiun said, "or else remove it from the wall. I cannot stand all this interruption when I am trying to write a history for the people of Sinanju."

Remo glanced at Chiun on the floor, surround-

ed by sheets of parchment, quill pens, and bottles
of ink.

He answered the phone.

"Hello, Smitty," he said.

"Remo, this is Bobbi."

"What do you want? A fourth for doubles?"

"Remo, I'm frightened. I've seen men around
the front of my home and they look like the men
who were at Edgemont."

"Mmmmm," said Remo. He had sent Bobbi Delpheen home with orders to be careful, hoping he
would never hear from her again. Happiness was
never having to hear her Adidas tennis shoes
scuffling along the rug in his room.

"Can I come and stay with you, Remo? Please.
I'm frightened."

"All right," Remo said. "But be careful coming
here. And wear something warm. We're going on
a trip."

"I'll be right there."

Remo hung up with a grunt.

When he had sent Bobbi home, Remo had told
her to be careful. When he had sent Valerie home,
he had told her to be quiet. He wondered now if
she were being followed also.

"Hey, Chiun, you writing anything good about
me?"

Chiun looked up. "I am writing only the truth."

Remo was not going to stand there and be in-
sulted, so he called Valerie. He found her at the
desk in the museum.

"It's about time you called, freak," she said.
"When are you going to get rid of all that ... all
those ... you know, in the special exhibit room?

How long do you think this can go on? What do you think I am anyway?"

"That's nice. Have you had any problems? People looking for Willingham?"

"No. I put out a directive that he was going on vacation. But he can't stay on vacation forever. You've got to do something about it," she said.

"And I will. You have my absolute guarantee that I will," Remo said sincerely. "Have you seen anybody? Has anybody been following you?"

"Not that I know of."

"Have people been coming to see the exhibit?"

"No. Not since I've been back. I've kept the sign on the door that it's closed, but no one comes."

"And no one's been following you?"

"Are you trying to make me nervous? That's it, isn't it? You're trying to make me nervous. Probably to get me up to your room so you can have your way with me. That's it, right?"

"No, dear," Remo said. "That most certainly is not it."

"Well, don't think that some shabby trick is going to frighten me into going there. No way. Your silly maneuvers are transparent, do you hear me, transparent, and you can forget it, if, for a moment, you think you can frighten me and get me to—"

Remo hung up.

Valerie arrived before Bobbi, even before Remo was hanging up the phone from his conversation with Smith.

No, Smith had not heard anything about Joey 172. With the closing down of Folcroft, the flow of information to him had stopped, except for what he was able to glean from the newspapers. When he wasn't snowed in at his cabin.

No, he had not seen anyone around his cabin, and yes, the skiing was fine, and if he stayed on vacation another month, his instructor told him, he would be ready to leave the children's slope, and he would be happy to see Chiun and Remo if they came to Maine, but they could not expect to stay in his cabin because a) it was small and b) Mrs. Smith after all these years still had no idea of what her husband did for a living, and it would be too complicated for her to meet Remo and Chiun. And there was no shortage of motel rooms nearby, and what was that awful yawking in the room?

"That's Valerie," Remo said. "She calls that speech. You be very careful."

He hung up, just in time to wave down Chiun, who was turning threateningly on the rug toward Valerie, who had interrupted his concentration. Even now he was holding the writing quill poised on the tips of his fingers. In another split second, Remo knew, Valerie was going to have another appendage, a quill through her skull and into her brain.

"No, Chiun. I'll shut her up."

"It would be well if both of you were to shut up," Chiun said. "This is complicated work I do."

"Valerie," Remo said, "come over here and sit down."

"I'm going to the press," she said. "I'm tired of this. *The New York Times* would like to hear my story. Yes. *The New York Times*. Wait until

Wicker and Lewis get through with you. You'll think you were in a meatgrinder. That's it. *The Times.*"

"A very fine newspaper." Remo said.

"I got my job through *The New York Times*," Valerie said. "There were forty of us who answered the ad. But I had the highest qualifications. I knew it. I could tell when I first talked to Mr. Willingham." She paused. "Poor Mr. Willingham. Lying dead in that exhibit room and you, just leaving him there."

"Sweet old Mr. Willingham wanted to cut your heart out with a rock," Remo reminded her.

"Yes, but that wasn't the real Mr. Willingham. He was nice. Not like you."

"Swell," said Remo. "He tries to kill you and I save you and he's nice, not like me. Go to the *Times*. They'll understand you."

"Injustice," Chiun said. "You should understand it. You Americans invented it."

"Stick to your fairytales," Remo said. "This doesn't concern you."

The door to their suite pushed open and Bobbi came in. Her idea of cold weather garb was a full-length fur coat over a tennis costume.

"Hello, hello, hello, everybody, I'm here."

Chiun slammed a cork stopper into one of the bottles of ink.

"That's it," he said. "One cannot work in this environment."

"Were you followed?" Remo asked Bobbi.

She shook her head. "I watched carefully. No-body."

She saw Valerie sitting on the chair in the corner and looked absolutely pleased to see her. "Hello, Valerie, how are you?"

"Happy to see you dressed," Valerie said glumly.

Chiun blew on the parchment, then rolled it up, and stashed it and the quills and the ink into the desk of the suite.

"Fine, Little Father, you can finish that later."

"Why?"

"We are going to Maine."

"Blaaah," said Chiun.

"Good," said Bobbi.

"I'm going to get fired," said Valerie.

"Why me, God?" said Remo.

Chapter Thirteen

From Europe they had come. From South America and Asia they had come.

They had come from all over the world, the bravest of the Actatl. Their strengths had been wasted in misadventures before Jean Louis deJuin had assumed leadership of the tribe, and this was what was left.

Twelve men, wearing the yellow feathered robes and the loin cloths, stood barefooted in ankle-high snow, oblivious to the cold, looking down a hill at a small cabin nestled in a stand of trees.

The cold Maine mountain wind whipped around them, and the gusts flattened the feathers of their robes against their bodies, but they neither shivered nor shook because the ancient traditions had held it that a child could not become a warrior until he had conquered a snake and a jungle cat and the hammer of the weather, and despite the passage of twenty generations all of them, even fat old Uncle Carl, knew they were Actatl warriors, and that warmed them and gave them strength.

They listened as one now as Jean Louis deJuin, dressed in heavy leather boots and a hooded fur parka, gave them their instructions.

"The woman is for sacrifice. The man I must speak to before we offer him up to Uctut."

"Will those two, the white man and the Oriental, come?" asked Uncle Carl.

DeJuin smiled. "If they do, they will be killed—from within their own encampment."

Chapter Fourteen

Mrs. Harold W. Smith was frumpy.

At thirty-two, she hadn't known it; at forty-two, she had known it and worried about it; and now, at fifty-two, she knew it and no longer cared about it.

She was, she often reminded herself, a grown woman and would act like one, and that included putting aside the childish fantasies about going through life doing exciting things with an exciting man.

So she didn't have that. She had something better. She had Dr. Harold W. Smith, and even though he might be dull, she no longer minded, because it was probably inevitable with all that dull work he did dull day after dull day at Folcroft Sanitarium, pushing dull piles of paper and worrying about dull educational studies funded by the dull federal government in Jacksonville, Arkansas, and Bell Buckle, Tennessee, and other dull places.

Harold—it wasn't Harry or Har, but Harold. Not only did she always call him Harold, but she had always thought of him as Harold. Harold might have been a far different man, she often thought, if he had simply been placed in different circumstances.

After all, in World War II he had done some kind of secret work, and while he would never say anything more about it than that he had been "in codes," she had once run across a personal letter from General Eisenhower, apologizing that circumstances made it impossible for the United States to award Harold W. Smith the Congressional Medal of Honor, adding that "no man who served on the side of the Allies deserved it more."

She had never mentioned to her husband that she had found this letter inside the front cover of a book on a shelf over his desk. To discuss it might have embarrassed him, but she often thought he must have been exceptional "in codes" to have merited such praise from Ike.

The day after discovering the letter she got to worrying that she might not have returned it quite exactly to its spot inside the cover of the book, and she went back to look at it again. But it was gone, and in the ashtray in his study she had found bits of burned paper—but that couldn't have been it. What kind of man would destroy a personal letter of praise from a man who went on to become President of the United States?

No one would do that.

She listened to the coffee percolating on the stove, filling the small kitchen of their rented Maine cabin with the oily sweet smell of coffee, on which she had come to depend to start the day, and she regretted nothing.

Harold might be, yes, admit it, dull, but he was also kind and a good man.

She turned off the electric burner and took the pot off the hot grill and placed it on the cool metal of the stove to stop the percolation and let the grounds settle.

It had been so nice of him to think about coming up here to Maine for a few weeks. She took two cups from a closet over the sink, rinsed them, and poured coffee into them.

She paused a moment.

Inside the bedroom she could hear Harold Smith's soft, methodical, regular breathing stop and surrender to a large sip of air, and then she heard the bed springs squeak. As he always did, Smith had awakened, had lain perfectly still for three seconds as if checking his surroundings, and then without any waste of time had clambered out of bed.

Seven days a week, it was the same. Smith never luxuriated in bed, not even for a moment, after he was fully awake: he climbed out as if late for an appointment.

Mrs. Smith carried the two cups back toward the small formica-topped kitchen table, glanced out the window, then stopped in her tracks.

She looked again, then set the two cups on the table, and walked to the window, pressing her face near the cold damp glass so she could see better.

That was odd, she thought. Definitely odd.

"Harold," she said.

"Yes, dear," he answered. "I'm up."

"Harold, come here, please."

"In a moment, dear."

"Now. Please."

She kept looking out the window and she felt Harold Smith move to her side.

"Good morning, dear," he said. "What is it?"

"Out there, Harold." She looked at the window.

Smith put his head close to hers and looked through the pane of glass.

Coming down the small slope of a hill toward the cabin were a dozen men, naked except for loincloths and feathered headdresses and robes.

They were dressed in the fashion of some sort of Indians, but they did not have the skin of Indians. Some were yellow, some white, some tan. They carried spears.

"What is it, Harold?" asked Mrs. Smith. "Who are they?"

She turned to her husband, but he was not there.

Smith had darted across the room. He reached up over the door and took down a .12 gauge shotgun that sat in a rack made of two sets of antlers. He locked the door's simple drop latch, then carried the gun to the small china closet in the room. From behind the dishes he took out a box of shotgun shells.

Mrs. Smith watched him. She had not even known those bullets were there. And why was Harold putting them in that gun?

"Harold, what are you doing?" she asked.

"Get dressed, dear," said Smith, without looking up. "Put on your boots and a heavy coat in case you should have to go out suddenly."

He looked up and saw her still at the window.

"Now!" he commanded.

Numbly, not really comprehending, Mrs. Smith moved toward their bedroom. As she stepped inside, planning to dress quickly, just to throw clothes on over the pajamas and robe she now wore, she saw Harold moving about the room, the shotgun folded in the crook of his arm like a hunter. He locked the windows of the small cabin, then pulled the curtains closed over the windows.

"Does it have something to do with the bicentennial?" she called as she slipped her heavy snow-pacs over her booted pajamas.

"I don't know, dear," he said.

Smith emptied the box of shells into the left pocket of his robe. Into his right pocket he placed a 9mm automatic that he took from a niche between the couch and the warm air radiator in the main living room.

He looked back into the bedroom. "Make sure that those windows are locked. Pull the curtains and stay in there until I tell you differently," he said, adding "dear" without meaning it. Then he slammed the bedroom door closed.

The dozen Actatl moved silently across the snow field toward the small house, nestled alone in the tiny valley alongside the hill.

On a snowmobile atop the hill, Jean Louis de-Juin watched as his men—his warriors, his braves—moved nearer the cottage. One hundred yards. Ninety yards.

He looked toward the snowed-over dirt road that cut its way through heavy pine growth to the cabin.

As the Actatl warriors moved nearer the house, deJuin saw what he had been expecting: a puff of snow coming along the dirt road to the Smith cabin.

A car.

This was it. The Actatl would win now or lose now. It was that simple. He smiled, for he had no doubt that the battle would be a victory for the Actatl.

Smith punched out a pane of glass from the kitchen window with the muzzle of his shotgun and put the barrel of the gun through the opening.

He sighted on the first of the feather-clad warriors, then coldly moved his aim toward the left, where a single shotgun blast might take out three men at once.

How long had it been since he had fired a gun? To kill? It all flashed through his mind in a split second, the days in World War II when he had to shoot his way out of a Nazi trap after he had spent four months in occupied territory in Scandinavia, organizing a resistance movement and training its members in sabotage, aimed at one target: the secret Nazi installation where heavy water experiments, needed to build an atomic bomb, were being undertaken.

A good cause then, a good cause now.

His finger began to tighten on the right trigger, but he stopped when he heard a car jerking to a stop before the front door of his cabin.

Was it more of them? Or was it Remo?

The door was locked. He would wait a moment. The warriors were now thirty-five yards away, stumbling ahead through heavy snow, and Smith again took dead aim.

At twenty-five yards he would fire.

Before he could squeeze the trigger, he saw a flash of color to the right of his window and then Remo, wearing only a blue tee shirt and black slacks, and Chiun, clad only in a green kimono, moved around the corner of the building and ran toward the dozen spear-carrying men.

The front pair of Indians stopped, set up quickly, and fired their spears. If Smith had not seen it with his own eyes, he would not have believed it. The projectiles sped toward Remo and Chiun. Both men seemed oblivious to them. At what seemed a fraction of a second too late, Remo's left hand moved before his face. The spear cracked in half and both parts fell harmless at his feet. He kept running toward the Actatl. The spear that went at Chiun seemed almost to have reached his stomach, seemed sure to penetrate, seemed certain to be deadly, when Chiun's long-nailed fingers reached down, and then Chiun was holding the spear in his own right hand. He had caught it in midflight.

164

Neither he nor Remo lost a step in their advance toward the Actatl. Then they were on them, and Smith realized that in all his years as the head of CURE, he had never before seen Remo and Chiun at work together. And as he watched them, he understood for the first time the terror that the Master of Sinanju and his disciple, Remo, could strike into so many hearts.

He understood too why Chiun believed Remo to be the reincarnation of the Eastern God, Shiva, the Destroyer.

Remo moved in a blur, in among the group of twelve warriors, who had stopped their charge on the house to dispose first of the two intruders. About Remo all was speed, as if he were surrounded by a special kind of turbulence, and bodies flew away from him as if they held a different magnetic charge from his and were thrust away by invisible forces.

While Remo charged into the center of the Actatl, Chiun worked around the perimeter of the group. His style was as different from Remo's as that of a rifle from a pistol. Chiun did not appear to move quickly; his hands and body were not blurred as he went from one spot to another. Smith noted almost scientifically that Chiun hardly appeared to be moving at all. But suddenly he was one place and then suddenly another place. It was like watching a film in which the camera had been stopped intermittently while shooting the picture, and Chiun's movement from one spot to the next had occurred while the camera lens was closed.

And the bodies piled up in a huge mound of yellow feathers, like some kind of giant canary graveyard.

Smith noticed another movement to his right and turned his head. A girl in a fur coat came around the corner of the cabin.

That would be Bobbi or Valerie, Smith thought. Bobbi, judging from the full length fur coat. She paused at the end of the cabin for a moment, watching as Remo and Chiun lay waste the Actatl warriors.

Not knowing she was being watched, she reached into the right pocket of her fur coat. She drew out a pistol.

Smith smiled. She was going to protect Remo and Chiun.

She raised the revolver at arm's length in her right hand. Smith wondered if he should call out to her and tell her to stop.

He glanced back at the battle. All the Actatl had fallen. Only Remo and Chiun still stood, ankle deep in the powdery snow. They had their backs to Bobbi. Remo pointed up to the top of a hill, where a man sat on a snowmobile, watching the carnage below. Remo nodded to Chiun and moved off in the direction of the man on the hill.

Smith glanced back at Bobbi. She extended her left hand and grasped her right wrist to hold the gun steady. She took deadly slow aim across the twenty feet between her and Remo and Chiun.

She was going to shoot them.

Smith wheeled in the window opening, moving to his left, and without aiming squeezed first the right trigger of his shotgun and then the left.

The first blast missed. The second caught Bobbi in the midsection, lifted her in the air, folded her as if she were a dinner napkin, and set her down into the snow eight feet from where she had been standing.

Remo turned, saw Bobbi lying on the snow, blood oozing out of her almost severed midsection, melting the snow where it touched it, creating a purplish brown paste. He looked at the window where Smith still held the gun.

"Nice work, Smitty," Remo said sarcastically. "She's with us."

Smitty passed by the bedroom door on his way outside. He called to his wife, "Stay inside there, dear. Everything's going to be all right."

"Are you all right, Harold?"

"I'm fine, dear. Just stay in there until I call you."

Smith put the gun against the wall and went outside onto the porch, which wrapped around the small cabin.

Remo looked up at him and laughed.

"What's so funny?" Smith said.

"Somehow I had this idea you slept in a gray suit," Remo said, gesturing toward Smith's pajamas. "I thought you always wore a gray suit."

"Very funny," Smith said.

Chiun was leaning over the girl. When Remo and Smith approached, she hissed to Remo: "You are one with the despoilers of the stone. You must die."

"Sorry, but it doesn't look like you're going to be able to carry it off," Remo said.

"She was trying to shoot you," Smith explained.

"She wouldn't have," Remo said.

"You had your back turned."

"What has that got to do with it?" Remo asked. He knelt closer to Bobbi. "What's your interest in all this? Just because I wouldn't play tennis with you?"

"I am a daughter of Uctut. Before me, my father and before him, his father, through many generations."

"So you helped them kill your own mother?" Remo said.

"She was not of the Actatl. She did not protect the sacred stone," Bobbi said. She sipped air heavily. It gurgled through her throat.

"Who's left to protect the stone now, kid?" Remo asked.

"Jean Louis will protect it and he will destroy you. The king of the Actatl will bring you death."

"Have it your way."

"Now I die with the secret name on my lips." She spoke again, and Remo leaned close and heard the secret name of Uctut as she spoke it. Bobbi's face relaxed into a smile, her eyes closed, and her head fell to the side.

Remo stood up. Lying on the ground in her fur coat, surrounded by bloody slush, she looked like an oversize muskrat lying on a red pillow.

"That's the biz, sweetheart," Remo said.

Remo looked up toward the hill. The man on the snowmobile was gone.

"Oh, my god! Oh, my god!" Remo turned. The
168

new noise was Valerie, who had finally worked up nerve enough to come see what was happening after having heard the shots.

She stood at the corner of the cabin, looking at the bodies lying about the snowfield.

"Oh, my god! Oh, my god!" she said again.

"Chiun, will you please get her out of here?" Remo asked. "Muzzle her, will you?"

"I do not do this thing because it is a command," Chiun said. "I do not take commands from you, only from our gracious and wise emperor in his pajamas. I do this thing because it is so worth doing."

Chiun touched Valerie on the left arm. She winced and followed him back to the car.

"Well, you've got to get rid of these bodies," Smith said.

"Get rid of your own bodies. I'm not the dog-warden."

"I can't get rid of the bodies," Smith said. "My wife's inside. She'll be nosing around in a minute. I can't let her see this."

"I don't know, Smitty," Remo said. "What would you do if I weren't around to handle all these details for you?"

He looked at Smith, self-righteously, as if demanding an answer that would not come. Remo went to the shed near Smith's front door and dragged out Smith's snowmobile. Every cottage and cabin in this part of the country came with one because the snow sometimes was so deep that people without snowmobiles could be cut off for weeks. And having guests freeze to death or die of starvation did nothing for Maine's tourist business.

Remo started up the snowmobile and drove it to the pile of corpses, which he tossed onto the back of the ski-equipped vehicle like so many sacks of potatoes. He put Bobbi Delpheen on the top and then used some random arms and legs to tuck everybody in so they wouldn't shake loose.

He turned the snowmobile around, aiming it toward the top of a hill, which ended at a big gulley with a frozen river in its bottom, then cracked the steering mechanism so the snowmobile's skis could not turn. He jammed the throttle and jumped off.

The snowmobile lumbered away up the hill, carrying its thirteen bodies.

Remo said to Smith, "They'll find it in the spring. By that time, you do something to make sure no one knows who rented this place."

"I will."

"Good. And why don't you go back to Folcroft? No need for you to keep hiding here."

Smith glanced up the hill. "What of the king of this tribe?"

"I'll take care of him back in New York," Remo said. "Don't worry."

"With you on the job, who could worry?" said Smith.

"Damn right," said Remo, impressing himself with his own efficiency.

He looked around at the blood-stained snow, then picked up a loose yellow feather and began brushing snow around to cover the stains. In a few seconds, the yard looked as pristine as it had before the start of the battle.

"What about Valerie?" Smith said.

"I'll keep her quiet," Remo said.

He walked away. A moment later Smith heard the car's motor start and begin to move away.

Smith waited a moment before reentering his house. He paused inside the front door and yelled out at the empty open countryside: "That's enough fooling around. If you fellas want to practice your games, go somewhere else. Before somebody gets hurt. That's right. Get moving."

He waited twenty seconds, then closed the front door, and went into his bedroom.

"You were right, dear," he said. "Just some fools practicing war games for the bicentennial. I chased them."

"I heard shots, Harold," Mrs. Smith said.

Smith nodded. "That warned them off, dear. I fired off into the trees. Just to get them moving."

"The way you were acting before, I thought there was really something dangerous happening there," Mrs. Smith said suspiciously.

"No, no. Nothing at all," Smith said. "You know what, dear?"

"What?"

"Pack. We're going home."

"Yes, Harold."

"These woods are boring."

"Yes, Harold."

"I don't think I'll ever be a good enough skier to get off the children's slope."

"Yes, Harold."

"I feel like getting back to work, dear."

"Yes, Harold."

When he left the room, Mrs. Smith sighed. Life was dull.

Dull, dull, dull.

Chapter Fifteen

Across the river from New York City, in Wee-
hawken, New Jersey, is a small exercise in con-
crete called a park, which commemorates the
murder of Alexander Hamilton by Aaron Burr.

The park is a postage stamp alongside a bumpy
boulevard that snakes its way along the top of the
Palisades, and it is supposed to commemorate the
spot where Hamilton was shot, but it misses by
some two hundred feet. Vertical distance.

Hamilton was shot at the foot of the Palisades
cliff, down in a rock-strewn area of rubble and de-
bris that used to be cleaned up regularly when the
ferry to Forty-second Street in New York was
running. Since the closing down of the ferry, it
had been ignored.

So it was hardly likely that one more rock in that area would have captured anyone's attention.

If it had not been for Valerie Gardner.

After making good on his promise to clear the bodies of Willingham and the other dead Actatl out of the special exhibit room at the museum, Remo had found a way to put Valerie's big mouth to good use.

And while she still thought he was a homicidal maniac, he had explained carefully to her that a successor would soon have to be named for Willingham, and who would have a better shot at the job than the young female assistant director who had worked so hard to preserve museum property?

So after Remo had contracted with a special moving company in Greenwich Village, which was used to working at night because it specialized in getting people and their furnishings out of apartments between midnight and five A.M., when landlords slept, Valerie got on the telephone with the representatives of the New York TV stations, the newspapers, wire services, and news magazines.

At one o'clock the next afternoon, when the gentlemen of the press arrived at the rock-littered site of the Hamilton-Burr duel, they found Valerie Gardner and a giant eight-foot stone, carved with circles and awkward birds, which Valerie informed them had been kidnapped from the museum and held for a "sizeable ransom," which she had paid personally, since she had not been able to contact the director, Mr. Willingham, for authorization.

A strong north wind blew in the face of the

stone statue, as Valerie explained that it was the ritual god "of a primitive Mexican tribe named the Actatl, a tribe which distinguished itself by vanishing absolutely with the arrival of Cortez and his conquistadores."

"Any leads on who took the stone?" one reporter asked.

"None yet," said Valerie.

"How did they get it out of the museum? It must weigh a ton," another reporter asked.

"Four tons," said Valerie. "But our guard force was depleted last night because some of our men were ill, and the burglars were able to break in and remove this, probably with a fork lift truck."

The reporters asked some more questions, while cameramen took film of Valerie and the stone, and finally one reporter asked, "Does this thing have a name? How do we refer to it?"

"To the Actatl, it was god," Valerie said. "And they called it Uctut. But that was its public name. It had a secret name known only to priests of the Actatl."

"Yeah?" said a reporter.

"Yes," said Valerie. "And that secret name was . . ."

Cameras whirred almost noiselessly as Valerie spoke the secret name of Uctut.

The case of the kidnapped stone was on the press wires and on the television all over the country that night. And across the country, even around the world, people who believed in Uctut watched as Valerie spoke the sacred name. And when the skies did not darken, nor the clouds fall, they sighed sadly and began to think that perhaps, after almost five hundred years in the west, they should stop thinking of themselves as Actatl, a hardly remembered tribe that worshiped a powerless stone.

But not everyone saw the broadcast on television.

After Valerie and the reporters had left, three men stood at the park atop the Palisades looking down at the huge monument.

In the center, looking down upon Uctut, was Jean Louis deJuin, who smiled and said, "Very clever. But of course it was all clever. How did you find me?"

The man to his right answered.

"Your name was in Willingham's files," Remo said. "All the names were. You were the only Jean Louis, and that was the name Bobbi gave me."

DeJuin nodded. "Information will be the death of us all yet." He looked to the old Oriental at his left side.

Chiun shook his head. "You are an emperor and this is what you get for not hiring qualified help. Entrusting serious business to amateurs is always a mistake."

"Now what is to happen?"

"When this is all on the news tonight," Remo said, "sacred name and all, the Actatl will see that Uctut's a fake. And that's that."

"And your secret organization will just pick up the pieces and continue as before?" deJuin said.

"Right," Remo said.

"Good," said deJuin. "Done is done and over is over. I don't think I was ever really cut out to be a king. Certainly not king of people who worshiped a rock."

He smiled, first at Remo, then at Chiun, as if sharing a private joke with them.

They did not smile back. Remo thrust a hand into deJuin's pocket, leaving there a piece of paper. And Chiun threw deJuin off the cliff down onto the statue of Uctut, which deJuin hit with a splat.

"Good," Chiun said to Remo. "Over is over and done is done."

DeJuin's body would be found that evening by sightseers who watched the news item on television and hustled to the foot of the Palisades to see the big stone.

Police would find in deJuin's pocket a typewritten note that admitted that he had planned and carried out the murders of the congressman, Mrs. Delpheen, and Joey 172; in retribution because they had not prevented the stone Uctut from being defaced. The note would also say that Uctut was a false god, and that Jean Louis deJuin, as king of the Actatl, renounced the ugly hunk of rock and was taking his own life in partial penance for his part in the three savage, senseless murders.

The press would cover all these events thoroughly, just as thoroughly as they would ignore the return to Folcroft Sanitarium of Dr. Harold W. Smith, sanitarium director, well rested after his vacation trip to Mount Seboomook in Maine and now busy revamping the sanitarium's sophisticated computer system.

And Remo and Chiun would sit in their hotel room and argue about dinner.

"Fish," said Chiun.

"Duck would be nice," Remo said.

"Fish."

"Let's have duck. After all it isn't every day we kill a king," said Remo.

"Fish," said Chiun. "I am tired of looking at feathered things."